TAKEN FOR THE TIGER

A NOVEL BY

ANNABELLE WINTERS

Books by Annabelle Winters

The CURVES FOR SHEIKHS Series

Curves for the Sheikh
Flames for the Sheikh
Hostage for the Sheikh
Single for the Sheikh
Stockings for the Sheikh
Untouched for the Sheikh
Surrogate for the Sheikh
Stars for the Sheikh
Shelter for the Sheikh
Shared for the Sheikh
Assassin for the Sheikh
Privilege for the Sheikh
Ransomed for the Sheikh
Uncorked for the Sheikh
Haunted for the Sheikh
Grateful for the Sheikh
Mistletoe for the Sheikh
Fake for the Sheikh

The CURVES FOR SHIFTERS Series

Curves for the Dragon
Born for the Bear
Witch for the Wolf
Tamed for the Lion
Taken for the Tiger

The CURVY FOR HIM Series

The Teacher and the Trainer
The Librarian and the Cop
The Lawyer and the Cowboy

TAKEN FOR THE TIGER

A NOVEL BY

ANNABELLE WINTERS

2019
RAINSHINE BOOKS
USA

Copyright Notice

Cover Design by S. Lee

ISBN: 9781075400896

0 1 2 3 4 5 6 7 8 9

TAKEN FOR THE TIGER

1
<u>CHAOS AT THE CIRCUS</u>
<u>CASABLANCA, MOROCCO</u>

Taken! I'm being taken by a tiger!

Tracy's bobcat snarled as she felt the tiger's jaws close around the scruff of her neck, lifting her clean off her feet like she was a fluffy little kitten. But she wasn't a kitten, and she tried to twist in the air and claw the tiger's eyes out as the massive Shifter broke into a graceful run, bursting through the velvet curtains behind the circus with her in his mouth.

"Put me down!" hissed Tracy, trying again to desperately claw at him. But of course nature had made it impossible for a cat being carried by the scruff of its neck to turn that way, and Tracy screamed in frustration as the scent of her twin sister faded while the tiger raced through the circus grounds. "Put me down and face me, you pussy!"

"Sorry. Can't do that," said the tiger. He had a British accent, and his voice was calm, steady, like melting butter, and Tracy felt it melt *her* like butter. Her bobcat purred in approval as Tracy gasped. Was her animal*enjoying* this? *Enjoying* being kidnapped by a Shifter four times its size?!

We aren't being kidnapped, purred her bobcat. *We're being taken. Taken by our mate. Meow! Meeeeeee—owwww!*

Our mate?! Our *mate*?! OMG, our *mate*! Tracy thought as she felt the truth of what her bobcat had just whispered. She'd teased her twin about the two of them finding their mates in the romantic city of Casablanca, and now here she was, being carried across the threshold by a British Tiger Shifter with a voice like butter!

"Where are you taking me?" she asked, doing her best to control the excitement that was ripping through her cat's body. She couldn't turn and fight while being held like this anyway, so she might as well talk.

But the tiger didn't answer. He just kept going, barreling ahead until the circus grounds were left in his dust. They were on the outskirts of the city, and Tracy turned her head as far as she could to see what lay before them.

"Um, I think that's the ocean," she said, her cat's eyes going wide as the smell of sea-salt floated over on the breeze. "Are you crazy? We'll both drown!"

"Tigers are excellent swimmers," said the Shifter. "How about bobcats?"

"Cats don't do water," hissed Tracy. "Turn around, please. Take me back to my sister."

The tiger grunted, slowing down as it got to the beach, its breathing still calm and controlled, its heartbeat steady like a drum. "There's no going back. Your sister will be safe with Darius. And you'll be safe with me. We're your mates. You know that, don't you?"

Tracy blinked, staring down at the golden sand of the beach as the tiger carried her along like she was a doll. Did she know it? Of course she did! But that still wasn't a good reason to be separated from her twin, was it? There was *no* good reason to be separated from her twin. Not one. Not even this. Not even *him*.

"Who were those men?" Tracy asked suddenly as the memory of those silent men who smelled like Shifters came back to her. Yeah, they smelled like Shifters, but Tracy couldn't figure out what kind of animals they were! It was strange as hell. Confusing as hell. *Terrifying* as hell!

"Shifters," said the Tiger, a grimness in his voice.

"Tell me something I don't know," growled Tracy, staring at the sand moving beneath her as the tiger carried her along. "And put me down, please. I won't run."

"You're lying," said the tiger without breaking stride. "And I'm Everett, by the way."

Tracy sighed when she realized that yeah, she was lying. Hell yeah, she'd run! Right back to her twin sister! She sighed again, and then she snorted. "Everett? That's quite a sophisticated name for a grungy, orange-striped beast. Your parents must have been comedians."

The tiger's jaws opened immediately, and Tracy felt herself drop onto the hard-packed sand with a thud, her bobcat landing on its ass. "Ow!" she snarled, about to leap onto all fours to face her annoyingly calm captor. Or mate. Mate! OMG, he's my mate!

But Tracy couldn't get up, because the Tiger was standing above her, eyes blazing deep orange, teeth long and sharp, startlingly white, like they'd been carved out of ivory by the gods themselves. He was beautiful, and although she hadn't seen him as a man yet, she could feel the man inside him.

Good, purred her bobcat. *Because soon he will be inside you. Can we Change back now, please? That's enough getting-to-know-you nonsense. Change back to the woman, turn around, and arch your back down and raise your ass like in that video we watched last month.*

"What video?" Tracy muttered, frowning as she felt herself turn bright red—if that was even possible for a bobcat. Then her eyes went wide when she remembered—well, *kinda* remembered—

what her cat was talking about: A drunken night when she'd pulled up some filthy video on Lacy's computer, sending both girls rolling around the floor with laughter as they watched some amateur actress pretend like she was actually enjoying whatever the hell the guy was doing with his—

"What's your name?" came Everett's voice from above her, and it took Tracy a moment to blink herself back to reality. Or whatever strange version of reality this was—with her being pinned down by a Tiger Shifter on a beach in Casablanca.

"What?" Tracy whispered, feeling her cat mewling as it tried to retreat so the woman in her could come out.

"Your name," said the Tiger, grinning wide as it leaned in close and sniffed her like it could maybe smell her name out. Was that possible? Who the hell knew! Tracy hadn't even seen another Shifter before today! "You have one, don't you? Or do you and your sister just use pronouns to refer to one another?"

"Pronouns? Do you even know what that means?" Tracy retorted, still on her back but now feeling a strange warmth roll through her body. Somewhere in the back of her mind she knew she should be anxious, worried, tense, freakin' the hell out after what had happened at the circus! Hell, her twin was missing! But she was feeling oddly calm, as if the tiger's sense of supreme control was infecting her in the most beautiful way, making her believe that everything was all right, everything was perfect, everything was . . . meant to be?!

Fate, whispered her bobcat impatiently. *Congratulations, genius. Now can we get on with it? We are in heat, and the time is ripe.*

"The time is *ripe*? Ew! Don't you mean the time is *right*?" muttered Tracy under her breath.

Whatever, snickered her bobcat. *You know what I mean.*

"Are you talking to your animal?" Everett said from above her, his warm breath making her whiskers flutter. "You know you can do that in your mind, don't you? Inside voice. It's very confusing when I'm asking you questions. Questions that you haven't bothered to answer yet, I might add. Where I come from, that's considered rude."

"And where I come from, *kidnapping* is considered rude!" snarled Tracy even though she was smiling inside, that feeling of warmth and security spreading through her like the sun breaking through the clouds.

"A Shifter taking its mate is not kidnapping," said the Tiger with a grunt. "And when he's also saving her furry bum, it's considered heroic."

"Oh, so you're a hero now?" Tracy said.

"Yes," said the Tiger, his eyes twinkling as he sniffed her again and then slowly backed away so she could get on all fours. "Now, are you going to run if I let you stand?"

"I dunno," Tracy said. "We'll have to see, won't we?"

"Dunno? Is that a word in the English language?" said the tiger, one eyebrow raised.

"Where I come from, yeah. It is." Tracy finally stood, her tail slowly moving from side to side as she looked up at the massive tiger standing before her. She wasn't going to run, and they both knew it.

The sound of the ocean came to her as the waves rolled in from her left. Her bobcat dug its claws into the sand and growled softly. It didn't like the water. Not one bit. It was a mountain cat, and although the Rockies had streams and rivers and waterfalls, she'd always kept her distance, kept her fur dry.

"Eliza," said the tiger firmly, one eyebrow still raised. Then it grunted and nodded. "Yes, Eliza. That's your name."

Tracy just stared, cocking her head as her claws dug deeper into the sand. "Wait, did you just . . . just *name* me?"

Everett shrugged. "I asked you your name. You didn't answer. I don't ask twice. Eliza is now your name."

"OK, that's just beyond rude! You can't just *name* someone! And why the hell am I Eliza? Is that some ex of yours?"

"Eliza Doolittle from *Pygmalion*," said Everett with a grin. "You know, the famous play by George Bernard Shaw? It's about a sophisticated Englishman who teaches a rude, uneducated girl how to speak the Queen's English." His grin broke wider. "He also teaches her some manners."

Tracy stared up at him, not sure if she was being insulted or teased. Perhaps both. She was about to snarl out a cocky response, but then the tiger just turned and walked away from her, heading straight for the ocean! She stared at the magnificent animal, wondering if she was dreaming or maybe even dead. Was he going to just disappear into the ocean like some mythical sea monster?! Had years of tequila and loneliness finally rotted her brain from the inside out?!

"Um, you know I'm not following you in there," she called after him, surprised at the hint of hope in her voice, like she wanted him to turn back and come bounding over to her.

"Don't worry, Eliza," he shouted over the roar of the waves. "You won't get your pretty little paws wet. I have a boat."

He has a boat, whispered her bobcat like that suddenly made it all OK.

"OK, having a boat does not make this a good plan—whatever the hell your plan might be," snarled Tracy. "Two cats on a boat? Is this a horror story or a romance?"

"Have you ever read *Pygmalion*?" Everett called out as he walked right into the ocean. And just as the warm waters of the Moroccan coast lapped up against his orange fur, Everett Changed to the man, the transformation happening so smoothly and unexpectedly that Tracy purred out loud.

OMG, he's magnificent, she thought as she felt her jaws hang open at the sight of her mate from behind. He was tall and broad, with thick black hair that kissed his shoulders as he stepped into the ocean. His back was like a pit of bronze snakes, the muscles shining in the sun as he bent over and reached for a boat that she hadn't noticed before. Of course, she didn't give a damn about the boat, because the sight of his naked, muscular ass flexing as he pulled the vessel up on the beach made her almost faint as her cat thrashed and mewled with pent-up frustration that was making it hard for Tracy to stay in animal form.

"No," she muttered, blinking as she suddenly remembered his question. "I haven't read *Pygmalion*. What happens when the sophisticated Englishman teaches the rude country girl some manners?"

Everett pulled the long, wooden boat up onto the beach and then turned to her, straightening his body and rising to full height. He was naked as the day, but completely without shame or embarrassment. In fact he was carrying himself with an elegance that Tracy was sure he'd display even if he were wearing a fitted tuxedo. He stood there in the sun, his yellow eyes burning with the fire of his tiger, one arm resting on the bow of the boat, his long cock hanging down between his legs in the most beautiful way.

And then Tracy felt herself Change back to the woman, her own transformation coming through with a powerful gentleness that she knew couldn't be stopped. Her breath caught as a sudden rush of fear whipped through the woman in her. Would he like what he saw? Oh, God, why hadn't she cut back on carbs the past month like she said she was gonna do?! Would her mate be repulsed by her fat thighs and big butt?!

But Everett just gazed at her, a slow smile breaking on his handsome face. With a flick of his eyes that Tracy knew was involuntary, like he couldn't help himself, he took in her nakedness, and Tracy felt her heat rise when she saw how his cock filled out and stood straight up in a way that couldn't hide how goddamn aroused he was. Immediately all her self-consciousness faded away, her insecurity disappearing as her feminine heat made her shudder with warmth. He was her mate, and she was his. She knew it. She felt it. She wanted it.

"In the story, the sophisticated Englishman sees her for the woman she is, the woman she always was," Everett said quietly, his eyes narrowing as he looked at her with a mix of playfulness and the most devastating sincerity. "And then he falls in love with her—rudeness, bad grammar, and everything else be damned."

Tracy felt her bare feet move as his words sent a ripple of warmth through her naked body, making her buttocks tense up as she caught a whiff of her own sex, felt her wetness begin to ooze from her slit. The warm waters tickled her toes, but it didn't bother her. She couldn't stop moving towards him if she tried. She'd been taken by the tiger, and now all she wanted was to be taken again. Taken forever.

She could see his cock throb as she got close, and when his masculine scent invaded her senses, Tracy knew she was ready. Her cat was purring like a wild beast in the background, taking delight in the woman about to do what had seemed would never happen. Her vision blurred as images of the two of them locked in embrace formed with a clarity that made it seem more than real, a vividness that made her moan out loud.

Then she was up against him, and she could feel his hardness against her naked belly, his cock pressing against her dark feminine triangle lengthwise as he leaned in for a kiss, their first kiss, *her* first kiss. The first one that mattered, anyway. The only one that mattered.

He kissed her hard and he kissed her deep, with an authority that she knew came from the stars above, the earth below, the open ocean, the endless sky. The kiss seemed to last forever, and it was only when her head began to spin from holding her breath did she pull away and gasp.

He held her tight, smiling as her chest rose and fell against his. His lips were so close she could feel his breath on her nose and mouth, and she grinned in delight when she realized how crazy and wonderful this was! He didn't even know her name, but yet they knew they were mates, that they were fated to be together, to grow old together, to live and die together.

A spark of pure electric magic seared her from the inside as their lips touched again, and Tracy's eyelids fluttered as she felt Everett's hand cradle her neck, tightening as he pulled her closer, kissed her deeper, driving his tongue into her mouth as he pushed his hips against her crotch.

The waves of the ocean roared in the background, and Tracy smiled and opened her mouth wide to receive her mate's kisses. But then suddenly the sound of the waves was gone, like all the water had been sucked out of the ocean. Tracy blinked as she felt Everett pull back from the kiss, and then her eyes flicked wide open when she felt him go tight against her body.

"What's happening?" she gasped, blinking in

confusion as she tried to look past him at the ocean—which seemed to have mysteriously disappeared, leaving nothing but a wall of black.

A wall of black that was moving.

Moving towards them.

"Everett!" she screamed, her heart almost stopping when she saw two massive red eyes staring at them from the wall of black. This wall of darkness was a creature, she realized! Some kind of sea monster! With scales and tentacles and talons . . . and *wings*?! "It's a . . . it's a dragon! A *dragon*, Everett! We need to run! Everett? Everett? *Everett*!"

2

Everett felt the dragon's sharp wingtip pierce him from behind, driving right between his shoulder blades, deep into his tiger's heart. It didn't seem real, and he just frowned as he looked into his mate's big brown eyes. He could tell she was screaming his name, but he couldn't hear a damned thing. It was so quiet. So peaceful. So beautiful.

He smiled as he reached out to touch her face.

God, she was beautiful! Pretty round face like an angel's. Brown eyes that made him feel like he could see her soul, see the woman in her, the animal in her, the love in her. And curves that made his tiger purr like a housecat one moment, roar like the beast it was the next! Was she really his? Hell yes, she was! She'd always been his! She would always be his! Now and forever! In life and in death!

But then suddenly his senses returned, and his eardrums almost exploded when he heard the bloodcurdling screech of what could only be a dragon. He'd heard a dragon before—Murad's Black Dragon—so he knew what they sounded like. But this wasn't Murad. He knew the Sheikh's scent, and although this dragon smelled like the salt of the ocean, its native musk was female. Definitely female. A female dragon. Dark. Deadly. A cold killer.

"Everett!" came the scream of his mate, her voice cutting through the roar of the ocean. He just smiled at her, wondering why she was so upset. They'd found each other! This was their fate! There was nothing to worry about! That's what fate meant, right? Meant-to-be? Destiny? The inevitable!

But the pain ripping through his powerful body

seemed to be saying something else, and finally Everett followed his mate's horrified gaze and stared at the dragon's razor-sharp wingtip sticking out of his chest like the first shoots of spring. His heart was still pumping, but the blood was pouring down his bare chest and stomach as his mate howled and tried desperately to stop the bleeding with her hands.

"You'll cut yourself," he heard himself say through the blood-red dream world that seemed to be pulling him in, pulling him away from his mate, away from his fate. "Be careful, Eliza."

"My name's Tracy," she said, tears rolling down her cheeks as she tried to pull him away from the dragon's deadly barb. She was crying, but Everett could see the bobcat roaring inside her, its rage rising as if it was preparing to face this female dragon that had dared to interrupt a fated bonding! "And this dragon-bitch is about to get her red eyeballs ripped out. Hold on, Everett. Don't you dare die on me."

Wait, am I dying? Everett thought as he felt the real world slip away from him. He'd never believed he could die, and he didn't believe it now either. Yeah, he'd been stabbed through the heart, but he'd heal, wouldn't he? Sure.

"It's just a flesh wound," he grunted. "Just a

scratch. I'll handle this, babe. You get your arse out of here. Change now and run for it. Go find your sister. Find Darius. I should be fine by the time you get back."

But Tracy didn't Change into her bobcat, and Everett frowned when he saw the confusion in her eyes . . . confusion that was turning to panic.

"I . . . I can't," she stammered, her brown eyes going wide. "My cat won't come out! It's . . . it's not afraid. It just refuses to come out! I can't Change, Everett! I . . . I . . ."

She stopped speaking just then, and Everett roared when he felt the dragon's wingtip drive deeper through him like a spear, its sharp head effortlessly pushing into his mate as he watched like this was some horrible dream. He grabbed her arms and tried to push her away, throw her backwards so she could get to safety. But he felt her resist, felt her lean into him, like she didn't *want* to run, like she *couldn't* run, damned well *wouldn't* run!

"What are you doing?" he roared, his eyes burning bright as he tried to summon his tiger, call forth his animal, fight whatever was happening. But then he realized he couldn't Change either! Was it magic?! No. He knew what dark magic felt like—he'd experienced it being around Magda the Dark Witch. This wasn't magic. This was his Tiger straight-up refusing to come forth! What the hell was happening?! Had both their animals turned into pussycats when confronted by a dark she-dragon?

Relax, came his Tiger's inner voice just then, bringing back that strange, peaceful feeling that had washed over him when the dragon had first plunged its barb into him. *We have found our mate, and we can never die. Relax and follow your fate. We cannot fight a dragon with tooth and claw in the world of flesh and blood. But we can fight it from the world that lies beyond. Fight it from within. It is the only hope.* His animal paused, and Everett sensed that it was hiding something from him. *The only hope for all of us.*

And then Everett felt the air rush past him as the dragon pulled both him and his mate back towards the ocean, towards its open maws, swallowing them whole like they were morsels of meat on a skewer.

3

Tracy knew she should be panicking, but for some reason she was calm. Was this what death felt like? Dead calm? Maybe, she thought as the sun disappeared behind the dragon's open maws. She knew she'd been stabbed through the heart, but it felt like a pinprick. She'd felt Everett try to push her away, but running hadn't even crossed her mind. The thought of being separated from him scared her more than death, dragons, or anything in between. Wherever they were going, they were going together.

She looked up, her eyes widening at the sight of rows upon rows of savagely sharp teeth. Was this crunch-time, she wondered absentmindedly. Would Dragon-bitch fry her fat ass with dragonfire before eating her? Would she taste salty? Spicy? Would she give the dragon indigestion?

But the dragon's jaws stayed open, and Tracy frowned as she felt it slide its wingtip out of her and Everett like it was plucking a couple of cherries off a toothpick. The next moment it had closed its jaws and simply gulped them both down, whole and unbroken!

"What the hell!" Tracy shouted, not sure if she was terrified or exhilarated. She could feel herself tumbling head over heels, rolling down the dragon's massive gullet, her mate roaring as he tumbled alongside her. "Wheee!" she screamed, holding her arms up above her head like this was a roller-coaster in some surreal theme park of the underworld. "No hands!"

She heard Everett laugh alongside her, and she blinked in the darkness as she rolled to a stop, her body landing on his, the two of them deep in the dragon's gullet. It was pitch dark, but soon enough her bobcat's vision came to the rescue, and she grinned like a fool when she saw her mate's blazing eyes looking back at her.

"Are we dead now?" she asked, feeling his hands pull her close to his body. "I don't feel dead."

"I don't feel dead either," said Everett. "But I don't know what feeling dead feels like, so maybe we are dead. Ouch! Did you just pinch me? What the hell?!"

Tracy giggled as she pinched him again in the darkness. "Nope," she said. "You don't feel dead."

But as she spoke she realized that although the first pinch had felt like a pinch, when she did it again, Everett's flesh felt different. She blinked as she summoned more of her bobcat's night-vision, and then she almost cried out loud when she saw that her fingers were passing through her mate's thick arm like he was nothing but air, like he wasn't even there!

"But you *are* here!" she gasped, trying to touch herself and then realizing that shit, she was nothing but empty space too! She could see herself just fine, but she couldn't touch herself! She couldn't touch her mate! "What's going on, Everett?! Oh God, what's happened to us?!"

Everett seemed to have realized that they were now either spirits or holograms or something in between, and he clenched and released his fists, looking quizzically down along his naked body like he was trying to make sense of what they were, where they were, *who* they were, perhaps!

"We're mates, and we're together," he said firmly, looking up at the roof of the cavernous belly of the female dragon that had pierced their hearts and then swallowed them whole. "But I'm afraid we are indeed dead."

Everett's voice was calm and steady, and while earlier that voice had made her weak in the knees, right now Tracy almost lost it. She wanted a drink of warm tequila. She wanted the open mountains of Colorado. She wanted her sister. This wasn't how she envisioned her happily ever after. "OK, you need to stop talking like you're some British Professor of Dramatic Bullcrap!" she snarled, looking down at herself and realizing that the wound between her breasts was suddenly gone. That didn't surprise her. If her body was now just a figment of her imagination—or some manifestation of spirit-sauce or magic-dust or whatever—then sure, it made *complete* sense that the wound was gone and she was still dead! Why the hell not?!

Everett just raised an eyebrow as he stopped examining the innards of their new home in a dragon's belly. He looked down at Tracy and smiled. "Actually, I *am* a British professor. Well, I *was*—before Caleb the Wolf recruited me into Murad's Shifter Army." His smile widened and he shrugged again. "I taught World Mythology, which I suppose you could say is the study of ancient bullcrap. Stories made up by ancient civilizations all over the world." He took a breath— which seemed strange, since Tracy figured they didn't need to breathe—and turned in a slow circle, arms stretched out wide. "And this, my dear, is one of the oldest stories of them all."

Tracy sat down on her ass, crossing her legs as she wondered if she could summon up some clothes to hide her nakedness. Nope. No magic powers. No clothes. No . . . animal?

She frowned as she tried to summon her bobcat, but although she could feel it out there somewhere, still connected to her, still a part of her, it also felt like it was a world away, like in another dimension or something. A flash of panic went through her as she hugged herself. She couldn't call forth her animal?! She was alone?! Alone and dead!

You aren't alone, came the thought as she looked up at Everett, who was once again examining their cave like he was looking for a door or something. You're with your mate. A British Professor of Dramatic Bullcrap with a magnificent ass and a body you can't touch. Shit, this *is* hell, isn't it?!

"Well," said Everett, finally breaking away from the alluring gizzards of the mighty undersea lizard, "it appears we are indeed trapped inside a dragon."

"How can we be trapped if we're dead and have no bodies?" Tracy demanded, both eyebrows twitching as she frowned up at her mate who seemed infuriatingly calm. "Answer that one, Dr. Genius."

"Actually, I don't have a PhD," said Everett with a grin. "So you can't officially call me Doctor. Professor is fine, though."

Tracy closed one eye and scrunched up her face. "Wait, don't you need a PhD to be a college professor?"

Everett grunted. "Usually. But I just bullshitted my way into the job."

"So you're a fake professor. A liar. A fraud."

Everett shrugged, seemingly undisturbed by her accusations. "I'm a real professor. As for being a liar and a fraud: Guilty as charged. I *was* a liar and a fraud. I denied my true self for years, denied my animal nature, that other part of me. I devoted myself to expanding my mind while trying to hide from what my body was telling me about my true nature."

Tracy blinked, surprised at the ease with which Everett was opening up to her, revealing things about himself that most men would be ashamed to talk about—weaknesses, vulnerabilities, parts of themselves that were less than perfect. Who was this man? Tiger Shifter, British Professor who'd bullshitted his way into the job, soldier in some Shifter army?

"Who's Caleb the Wolf? What Shifter Army? Who's Murad?" Tracy said, the questions making her feel sick even though she shouldn't be feeling anything at all, right?

Everett opened his mouth to answer, but his voice was drowned out by a horrific screech that made the dark walls of their living cage shudder. It was the female dragon, and Tracy could feel its rage, hear its anger, sense its fury. The dragon had been quiet thus far, but something had riled it up. What?

"Murad is the Black Dragon," Everett said, frowning as he looked around as if something was just dawning on him—the same realization that was coming to Tracy. If Murad was a male Black Dragon and this was a female Black Dragon, then wasn't it possible that . . .

Again the dragon let out a cry that shook Tracy to the core, and she braced herself against the walls of its belly as it dove deep into the ocean. For a moment Tracy panicked, wondering if the dragon would open its mouth and swallow half the ocean, flooding its belly with saltwater, drowning her ass in like three minutes! But then she reminded herself that she was dead, and so she couldn't drown.

"How is it we can see each other, see our own bodies, but . . . but . . ." Tracy said when the dragon finally leveled off somewhere deep beneath the surface.

"But can't touch each other?" Everett said, his grin fading as he looked down along her body and then back into her eyes. He touched his own chest, frowning as if he'd suddenly realized that his own wound had disappeared too. "I don't know. I mean, we're clearly dead. But we're still here. Still conscious. Still . . . alive. Quite curious, really."

"Maybe we're hallucinating," Tracy muttered, rubbing her eyes and beginning to pace. She stared down at her bare feet as she walked along the floor of the dragon's belly. It looked smooth and clean. It felt cold. Lifeless. "I mean, if this is a dragon's belly, shouldn't there be all kinds of stuff in here? Fish, goats, bones, flesh . . . whatever it ate for lunch before swallowing us like strawberries? And where are its . . ."

"Innards?" said Everett, crossing his arms over his chest and then rubbing his chin thoughtfully. "This dragon's belly does seem awfully empty and surprisingly clean. Maybe it's on a purge. Some kind of new-age diet to cleanse itself?"

Tracy stared at Everett in disbelief. "Is that a joke? Do you really think this is the time and place to be making jokes?"

Everett shook his head. "No. You're right. We should be meditating on our sins."

Tracy's eyes went even wider. Who the hell was

this guy? Was her mate a madman? Was this hell? To be trapped for eternity with some British dude with a droll sense of humor?

"Please don't tell me you're some nutcase," she growled, clenching her fists and wishing she could reach her bobcat. Where was that feline, anyway? Was her animal dead too?! "I had enough of that growing up."

"Me too," said Everett, smiling and then looking up at the dark roof of their living cage. "Which is why I can't ignore the symbolism of what's happening to us."

"What symbolism?" Tracy said grumpily.

"You ever read the story of Jonah and the Whale?" Everett said softly, his eyes narrowing in a way that made it quite clear he wasn't joking.

"Dude gets swallowed by a whale? Sure. I vaguely remember it."

"It's a story that appears again and again in the world's mythology. It was in the oldest primitive mythology, and it's also part of the Hebrew Bible, the Christian Bible, and the Quran—the Holy Book of Islam," Everett said, his eyes shining with excitement.

Tracy paused when she looked into his eyes. She could see his intelligence like it was a living, breathing thing. He had a sharp mind, and clearly he took pride in it. Tracy was sharp-witted too, but she'd never paid much attention in class, never given a shit about grades or exams.

"I thought you didn't have a PhD," she said, raising an eyebrow. "That sounds pretty . . . um . . . *professorial*."

A shadow passed across his handsome face. "The only reason I don't have a PhD is because I lost my funding and was kicked out of the program."

"And why was that? You skipped class or something?" Tracy asked, suddenly interested in his past more than the puzzle of what the hell was happening to them.

Everett took a long, slow breath, his eyes shining with the energy of his tiger. Could *he* reach his animal, Tracy wondered. Could he Change and rip his way through this dragon? Oh, wait, no. They were dead. Oops.

"I probably *should* have skipped class that day," Everett said, his voice coming out as a low growl.

"Why? What happened? Ohmygod, did you Change into your tiger and freak everyone out?"

"I don't want to talk about it," growled Everett. "Can we get back to the topic at hand, please?"

"Actually, we don't *have* hands," Tracy retorted, swiping at him and marveling at how her seemingly solid right hand passed right through Everett. "Should we talk about that? OK. You first, Einstein."

"Jonah and the Whale," Everett said after clearing his throat pointedly. "So the story is that God gave Jonah a task, but he refused to do it. He denied his responsibility. Fled from his duty. And so—"

"Ohmygod, are you seriously giving me a lecture about some old parable?!" Tracy shrieked, closing her ears as if that would solve anything. "Can we focus on getting out of here, please?!"

"That's exactly what I'm doing," Everett said.

"No, you're not! You're totally denying the situation we're in! This isn't some intellectual puzzle that you can solve with your almost-PhD mind! We need to Change to our animals and rip our way out of this . . . this beast!"

"All right," Everett said, shrugging and then leaning against the dragon's belly like he was posing for *Gentleman's Quarterly*. "Go ahead and Change."

Tracy almost screamed again as she reached for

her animal and remembered she couldn't get to it.

"Can't do it, can you?" said Everett. "Me neither. I can feel my Tiger somewhere out there. But that's the point—it's *out there* while we're in here. We're just humans in here, Tracy. Human spirits. Man and woman. Whatever task that's been set for us has to be completed by the humans in us, without the help of our animals." Everett pushed himself away from the pulsating walls of their cage, his eyes once again shining with excitement. "Tracy, how old were you when you first Changed, when your animal first came forth?"

Tracy shrugged. "I dunno. Young. So young that I barely even remember my first transformation. My animal was always there. I was Changing back and forth almost before I could walk!" She frowned as she thought back. "In fact, I'm pretty sure my animal came forth before my sister's did. So much for her being the older one!"

Everett nodded. "Same with me. My first transformation happened when I was a kid too. My tiger's always been there. I've always had the strength and power of my animal. It made me reckless, made me believe I was invincible." He looked down at himself, blinking as if he was trying to come to terms with what they were. "I still believe I'm invincible," he said slowly, clenching and releasing his right fist like he was checking to see if he could feel himself. "I mean, we're not ghosts. I can clearly see my body." He looked up at her, taking a long, slow breath as he gazed upon her. "And I can clearly see your body," he whispered.

"Yes, clearly," said Tracy, placing her arm across her boobs even though it seemed silly if her boobs weren't really there. "Could you not stare like that, please?"

Everett blinked and looked away. "It's hard not to," he muttered, shaking his head as he began to pace. "You're my mate and I want to claim you. But I can't. *We* can't. We're forced to just sit here and . . . and*talk*!"

Tracy raised an eyebrow and put her hands on her hips. "I didn't realize talking to me was such a pain in the butt," she said hotly, even though she could feel her own frustration at being naked near her mate but unable to actually touch him, unable to feel his touch.

"That's not what I mean," growled Everett, his eyes narrowing as if his temper was rising along with his own frustration. The initial panic of what had happened on the beach was now giving way to the grim realization that this might well be hell or purgatory, a place where they'd be trapped for all eternity, unable to satisfy their basic needs. "I mean there's a reason this has happened to us. There's a reason this dragon swallowed us whole. We need to figure out what that is."

Tracy took a breath and nodded. "All right," she said softly. "Back to your story of Jonah and the Whale. So you're saying that God or the Universe or Fate or Destiny has put us in this spot for a reason. What's the reason? What's our task?"

"It has to be something we've denied about ourselves. Some responsibility that we've been hiding from," Everett said softly.

Tracy snorted. "Shit, I've been hiding from responsibility my entire life! Where do you wanna start?"

Everett chuckled. "All right. Maybe I'll go first." He paused, his grin fading as his expression darkened. "Though my life was also an exercise in avoiding responsibility. I just did what I wanted, when I wanted, without any real direction. Not until I joined Murad's Shifter Army. That gave me a purpose. It gave me a—"

But his words were drowned out by the dragon's

scream, and Tracy gasped when she realized this was the third time they'd mentioned the name Murad, and the third time this female dragon had almost gone berserk! She'd suspected it earlier, but now she was sure.

"OK, I think this is Murad's mate!" she shouted as the dragon turned and twisted beneath the ocean, tossing them around like ping-pong balls in its cavernous belly. "And she's pissed off about something." Tracy listened for a moment as the dragon's screams turned to what sounded like a droning wail. "Pissed off and . . . and . . . sad? Lonely? Maybe that's our task? To reunite this dragon with her mate?"

Everett snorted, and then he blinked in surprise as the dragon suddenly calmed down. He stared at Tracy, cocking his head and frowning. "Murad's mate," he whispered, slowly beginning to nod. "You might be onto something here. See how she calmed down when you talked about reuniting her with Murad?" But then Everett shook his head. "But this she-dragon would be able to find Murad on her own. She'd be able to seek out her mate without our help. Hell, I don't know where Murad is anyway! Why would it believe we have anything to offer?"

Because you are mated Shifters, came the answer from the dragon, its voice rumbling through the beast's body like thunder, making Tracy almost fall down in shock. *Mated Shifters can travel between Light and the Darkness. I am all Darkness. I cannot go to the Light. You can, and so I need you to go to the Light and do something for me. Find something for me. Carry a message for me.*

Tracy's eyes went wide as she stared at Everett. Suddenly she realized she was smiling, and Everett was smiling too! It was like they'd unlocked something, solved a piece of the puzzle!

"That was Jonah's task in the myth," Everett said as his smile widened. "To carry a message!"

But then her smile faded as she went over what the dragon had just said.

"Actually," she said, glancing at Everett as she thought back to that kiss they'd shared on the beach, "we aren't . . . *mated*. Not really. Not in the . . . um . . . *Biblical* sense at least."

You must be, whispered the dragon. *You were enveloped in Light. I was drawn to you both like a moth to a flame. Since my creation I have seen nothing but Darkness—seen nothing at all, in fact. Just black. Just dark. And then I was drawn to your light, and I had to possess it. Now go the Light. I cannot wait any longer. I am manifesting in the physical world, and I will consume it all as I yearn for balance. I will consume all the Light in the world unless you reunite me with my human, the human soul that was lost when Murad Turned me. Bring back the woman I once was, the mother I once was, the wife I once was. She is in the Light, and you two must bring her back to me. Now go. Go! GO!*

4

Go! Go! GO!

Everett felt a flash of the darkest despair go through him as he listened to the dragon speak. He could sense its turmoil, feel its anguish, almost *taste* its yearning for what it called the Light! He blinked as the pieces fit together in his mind: Tracy had guessed right! This *was* Murad's mate! But the dragon had said Murad had tried to Turn her! That . . . that wasn't possible!

"Dragons can't Turn humans," Everett muttered as he glanced at Tracy and saw that she was frowning hard as she tried to figure out what exactly this she-dragon wanted them to do—if they *could* do what it wanted them to do! "That's why the dragons are almost extinct. Any attempt to Turn a human simply results in death for the human."

"Well, that's what happened here too, it seems," Tracy said, still frowning. "But it also created a new dragon. So it *kinda* worked."

"Worked to create a wholly unbalanced Black Dragon," Everett growled, bracing himself against the smooth walls of the dragon's belly. "All Darkness. A dragon that's never been human. That *isn't* human." He shook his head, reaching once again for his Tiger that still seemed a world away—perhaps a million worlds away! "Tracy, a dragon that has never had a human side isn't a Shifter. It's a goddamn demon! We have to kill it! Destroy it! Send it back to Hell!"

Tracy shook her head furiously, her jaw tight, her pretty round face scrunched up as she thought. "It already *is* in hell, Everett! Don't you see? It's yearning to find its human, to connect with the woman that was lost when this beast was born! That means there *is* some connection to the Light! This poor dragon isn't all Darkness! There's hope for her!"

"Stop calling it a *her*!" Everett snapped. "This isn't a person. This isn't a woman. This isn't an animal! It's an abomination, a freak, a mistake of nature!"

"That's what humans say about us, you know," Tracy said, her eyes narrowing, her hands balling into fists. She was angry, he could tell, and so was Everett. He was about to snap back, but his words caught in his throat when he looked at his mate and suddenly realized he couldn't see her body clearly anymore! It looked misty, like it was fading!

"What the hell?" he muttered, looking down at himself as he realized that the same thing was happening to him! He was disappearing! "Tracy, do you see me?"

"No!" Tracy shrieked. "Hold me, Everett! Hold me! Oh, God, hold me!"

Everett roared as he tried to reach for his mate, but she was gone. And so was he. He'd never panicked before, but he was getting damned close to it as he roared again, shouting for his mate. He swore he could feel the dragon's anguish in that moment, and he wondered if this beast was some-how doing this!

He felt movement, like he was being pulled, and then Everett realized that he could still feel Tracy's presence. He couldn't see her or smell her or even hear her. But he could *feel* her. It was the strangest thing, but it calmed him down as he focused on that connection with his mate. Soon he realized that she was pulling him along, tak-ing him with her. They were indeed bonded—bonded by just one kiss! Nothing could separate them—not even death! Fate was real! Magic was real! Destiny was real!

Of course, we don't know what our destiny is yet, he reminded himself as he felt them being pulled somewhere, like they were rising through clouds, white clouds, shining with light brighter than the sun itself.

And then suddenly vision came rushing back, and he shouted in surprise when he landed hard on his arse, the smell of clean grass and healthy trees invading his senses even as it hit him that if he'd just landed on his arse and felt it, then he *had* an arse! A body! Had they been reborn? Had they come alive again? Did they wake from their hallucination?

"Everett!" he heard her scream, but now the

panic was gone from Tracy's voice. "Everett, look!"

He looked, his mouth almost hurting from how wide his grin broke, his heart almost bursting when he saw his mate in the flesh again, rolling around in a sea of green grass that glowed with what could only be the light of . . . of heaven? Was this where they were?

"Not quite," came a voice from Everett's left, and he whipped around to see who was talking. At first he didn't see anyone, but then he squinted and made out two shadowy figures walking towards them from a cluster of trees that looked strangely dark in comparison to what felt like light everywhere else.

"Who are you?" Everett growled, leaping to his feet and standing in front of his mate. He watched as a man and woman approached them. Both were tall and broad, and immediately Everett knew they were Bear Shifters. He sniffed the air, ignoring the delight he felt when he realized he had his sense of smell back. They smelled familiar. Yes, he knew that scent. It reminded him of Bart the Bear, who'd spent a year at Murad's castle, helping Caleb train the wild Shifters who'd been recruited into Murad's Army.

"Correct. We *are* related to Bart the Bear. We're his parents," said the woman with a smile. She was a large woman, with creases around her brown eyes and deep wrinkles lining her face. Everett wondered why anyone living in heaven would have wrinkles, but he blinked away the thought and moved closer to his mate. There was something strange about these two. They weren't evil, he could tell. But there was an unsettling darkness that lingered behind their tired eyes. It was like they hadn't slept in years. Like they were in a perpetual state of stress and worry. And what the hell was that curious cluster of dark trees from which they'd emerged? And why were there trees in heaven, anyway! And grass! And . . . and . . .

"In the Light, you see what you want to see," said Papa-Bear, his eyes flashing with a wistfulness that shook Everett. "What do you see?"

Everett frowned, feeling Tracy stand close behind him. He stood naked, but he could feel that Tracy had clothes on. Just a robe or a gown, but something that had spontaneously appeared. Sure, it made sense that she'd want to cover herself in the presence of strangers. Everett, of course, didn't give a damn about who saw him naked. In fact he thrived on freaking people out with his brazen self-confidence, his supreme delight in strutting around in his birthday suit.

Everett looked around, taking a slow breath as he savored the aroma of the wild savannah. "Tall, beautiful elephant grass. Green and yellow. Plains flat as my palm stretching for miles. A mighty river in the distance, flowing lazily through the even land."

"Um . . . no," said Tracy from behind him.

The two Bear Shifters smiled at each other and then glanced over at Tracy. "Tell him what you see," said Mama Bear.

Tracy stepped out from behind Everett, and Everett gasped when he saw her in the flesh, a yellow sundress covering her curves while revealing just enough to make him want to finish what they'd started on the beach in Morocco.

"Mountains," she said, spreading her arms out wide and making a slow turn, hesitating for a moment when saw him standing there naked and hard, shameless and proud. "Tall and thick, with beautiful peaks."

"Why, thank you," said Everett with a grin as he glanced down at his own peak. "What else do you see?"

"OK, we're with company," Tracy said, her round cheeks blushing red. "Can we . . . you know . . . not disgust them with your . . . um . . ."

"Don't worry," said Papa Bear, his eyes crinkling with amusement. "We also see what we want to see. Or, in this case, we *don't* see what we don't want to see."

"Your privacy is secure," said Mama Bear. "We see you as figures of light. As for what you two see of each other . . . well, that's your business."

"Excellent," said Everett, reaching out and sliding his fingers beneath the shoulder-straps of his mate's yellow sundress. He leaned close, feeling his need rise up so suddenly that he couldn't give a damn about these two Bear Shifters, didn't care about whether they were alive or dead, didn't want to know if this was heaven or hell or an alien spaceship. "So can we dispense with this sundress," he growled against her neck, inhaling her intoxicating scent as he felt his hardness push against her soft rear.

Tracy gasped, and Everett could smell her sex beneath her dress. He knew she was hot for him, wet for him, ready for him. He wanted to take her now. These bears could wait until they were done. This couldn't wait. The need was too strong. Too fierce. Unstoppable. Uncontrollable.

"Everett, are you insane?" Tracy whispered, pulling away from him even though he could tell it took some effort. "We don't know what's happening to us, where we are, *what* we are! And all you want to do is . . . is . . ."

"Go ahead," Mama Bear called out to them, her eyes narrowing as if she knew something they didn't. "We'll wait."

"We're very good at waiting," said Papa Bear, putting his arm around his mate's shoulder and posing like they were in a surreal postcard.

"We've been waiting for a long time," said Mama Bear, her voice dropping to a whisper as Everett felt his hand slide up beneath his mate's dress from behind, cupping her beautiful round bum as she backed up into him.

Everett's head began to spin as he felt his need take over. Tracy was whimpering out a protest, but he could tell she was being drawn by her need as well. The whole thing seemed oddly dreamlike, with those two bears standing there, arms around each other, waiting near those dark trees.

"You see mountains all around us?" Everett asked, suddenly remembering what Tracy had said earlier. "Seriously?"

"Yes," said Tracy, turning to face him, her eyes unfocused, like she was as confused as he about what was happening to their bodies, their minds, perhaps their souls. "Snow-capped mountains. Rolling foothills. Rocky terrain. Just like in Colorado. My home. My safe place."

"Your safe place is with me," Everett whispered, leaning in to kiss her but stopping just before his lips touched hers. His need to claim her was real, but it felt different than it had when he was in the flesh, on the hard sand of that beach, on the firm ground of Earth. What was this place? Was she really safe with him? Without his animal, could he protect her? Could he trust these odd bear-Shifters, even if they were Bart's parents? Not that being Bart the Bear's parents made them trustworthy—hell, hadn't he overheard Bart and Caleb talking about how Bart's parents had worked for the government in some secret research lab . . . working to *destroy* Shifters?!

"Kiss me," came Tracy's whisper through Everett's swirling mind, and when he blinked himself back into focus, he saw the need in her eyes. It wasn't so much the need of her body as much as it was a burning need to just find clarity, to reach for the one thing she could be sure of: Her mate. Her man. Her tiger.

Again he saw those two bear-Shifters standing in the background, patiently waiting like they'd been painted into the scenery. The more he thought about it, the less sense it made, and finally Everett just gave in, deciding to focus on the one thing *he* was sure of: His mate. His woman.

So he leaned in to kiss her, smiling as he anticipated how good her warm lips would feel against his. Hey, this was heaven, wasn't it? He saw the vast plains of the savannah, with elephant grass swaying in the breeze. She saw the snow-capped mountains of her home in Colorado. And those bears saw two figures bathed in cosmic light merging into one. Sure. That sounded like heaven. Go for it, Everett.

But the moment his lips touched hers, the background disappeared like a light had just gone out, and suddenly Everett found himself being pulled along with his mate . . . pulled like how they'd been pulled from the dragon's belly to the Light . . . except now it was along what seemed like a dark tunnel.

A tunnel to the Darkness.

"No!" Everett shouted, feeling the change in energy wash through both of them, a vision of those grinning bears sticking in his head as he held onto his mate as they turned and twisted in the air like feathers in the wind.

"Everett! What's happening?!" Tracy screamed, her arms tight around his body. But it didn't feel like her arms, Everett realized after a moment. It felt like . . . claws! Her bobcat's claws!

He roared in surprise when he realized they'd both Changed to their animals . . . Changed without knowing it, Changed without controlling it. He roared again, stretching his tiger's body and reaching for his bobcat mate as she snarled and hissed in surprise.

They landed on what felt like firm ground, and Everett crouched in front of his mate in a protective stance as he tried to get his bearings. It was pitch black where they were, darker than the darkest night he'd ever seen. He stayed quiet and listened, his tiger's big ears pricking up as a slew of distant sounds grew louder and louder until it was a cacophony of cries that seemed to come from everywhere.

"What is this place?" Tracy screamed, her bobcat turning around and around as the sounds of what felt like a million animals came closer and closer. "Everett! Where are you?!"

"I'm right here," Everett growled, dread rolling through his fearless tiger as he realized that he couldn't smell any of these animals. He could hear them all, sure: Bears, wolves, leopards, and everything in between. And now he could see their dark shadows whizzing through the blackness around them. But no scent. Strange as hell. Perhaps this *was* hell.

"Hello!" came a voice from somewhere above them, and Everett looked up and squinted through the darkness. "Hello! Hello! *Hello!*"

It was the two Bear Shifters, Everett realized as he made out the shadowy figures peeking down from what looked like the edge of a cliff far above them. They were both in bear form, and as Everett sniffed the air, he realized he could pick up their scent. He could smell his mate too. But the other animals . . . nope. Not a whiff of their natural musk! What were these creatures? Demons? Spirits? Ghouls? Goblins?

"Animals," came the answer from Mama Bear, her big bear's head looking down at him.

"Shifter animals," added Papa Bear, furrowing his furry brow.

"They have no scent," Everett shouted back up at them even though he suspected he didn't need to shout. These bears seemed to know exactly what he was saying, what he was thinking, what he was . . . feeling?

He glanced over at his mate as he wondered what she was feeling. Her bobcat was close to its tiger-mate, looking around skittishly as those semi-visible animals got closer and closer, their cries sounding like a jungle gone mad.

"We need to get out of here, Everett," whispered Tracy through her bobcat, and for the first time Everett sensed fear in this feisty cat. Real fear. Fear that was different from what he'd seen in her when the she-dragon had stabbed and swallowed them.

"I know," he said, trying to keep his voice calm. "We will. I just want some answers from these bear shifters first."

"Answers about what?" screamed Tracy through her cat as the wails and roars of the dark animals got closer. "This place? It's hell, Everett! It's hell, plain and simple! And we're in it! What did I do to deserve this? What sin did I commit to be sent here!"

"Stop talking crazy!" roared Everett, feeling himself begin to lose his nerve as the cacophony in the darkness grew louder, closer, like those animals were almost on them! There was nowhere to run, and Everett wondered if he'd be able to protect his mate down here! As a Tiger Shifter he'd been scared of nothing on Earth. But this wasn't Earth! This was somewhere else!

"It's you! You did this!" Tracy snarled, turning to him in the darkness, her bobcat's eyes blazing gold with anger. "We were in heaven, a resting place for souls! But you couldn't stop thinking about your body, about *my* body! And I . . . I gave in to temptation! Everett, we were in *heaven* and about to . . . to . . . to *fuck*! No wonder we're in hell now! You're a demon! You're the devil himself!"

Her bobcat leapt at him before Everett had a chance to reply, and his tiger roared in surprise as Tracy slashed him across the chest with her claws. He could feel his pain, smell his own blood, hear his mate's sharp claws and teeth rip away at him like she'd gone crazy. But more importantly, he could feel his mate's pain, her fear, her . . . her shame? Did she really believe they'd committed some horrible sin by giving in to their needs, to their desires, to their . . . love?! God, he didn't know this woman at all, did he? He knew she was his mate, but there was so much more he needed to know, so much more he *yearned* to know!

Everett covered his face with his mighty paws

as Tracy continued her attack. She couldn't do any serious damage, he knew. Tigers were some of the fastest healers of all Shifters. One wound would close up almost before her quick cat could open up another on his thick tigerskin. As for the pain . . . hah! It was nothing compared to that pain he suddenly felt deep inside, in his heart, in his damned soul! It was a yearning like he'd never felt before! A deep need to roam the beautiful earth with his mate, getting to know her, getting to know the *woman* in her! Yes, there was a need to claim her in the flesh, to take her the way his lust demanded, the way nature intended. He was part animal, and that was how an animal claims its mate.

"But for a man to truly claim a woman, he must know her heart, not just her body," Everett muttered out loud, blinking in the darkness. Were those words from some old book he'd read during his years as a lofty-minded graduate student at Cambridge? Was it divine understanding coming out of the ether itself? Perhaps it was those strange Bear Shifters, who seemed oddly poised at the threshold of good and evil, darkness and light, life and death. Like gatekeepers.

Everett stared up at those two lonely bears once again, and he frowned when he saw that they were smiling down at him.

"Now the tiger is getting it," said Mama Bear, folding her big paws across her chest and nodding. "He sees that mated Shifters can travel back and forth between the Light and the Darkness."

"Yes," said Papa Bear, rubbing his snout as he peered down. "He can see it, but he can't do it at will. One kiss was not enough to bond them fully. They can move between Light and Darkness, but without control. What a shame."

"Yes, shame," whispered Mama Bear, glancing at Tracy and then back at Everett, her eyes trying to tell him something. "The bobcat carries too much shame in her soul."

Papa Bear grinned. "And the tiger does not carry *enough* shame in his!" The Bear Shifter opened his snout wide and laughed, clapping his big paws together once. "What a shame."

"Shame, shame, shame," whispered Mama Bear, her eyes once again focusing on Tracy. "Shame. Shame. *Shame!*"

5
THIRTY YEARS EARLIER
DENVER, COLORADO

Shame! Shame! Shame!

Tracy blinked as she looked down at herself. Then she gasped when she looked up and saw the gaggle of schoolkids staring at her, pointing, laughing, jeering, mocking. It took her a moment to remember what had happened, and when it came back to her, she screamed and began to cry.

She'd Changed to her animal in the playground during recess! She'd Changed, but only for a moment. A flash of a second! Her young bobcat had burst forth and then almost immediately retreated back. Of course, even that instantaneous Change was enough for little Tracy to rip through her clothes, and before she knew it she was naked on the school playground, trying desperately to cover herself as the other kids pointed and laughed, howled and hooted, teased and tormented!

"Shame on you, Tracy!" came a teacher's stern voice, and Tracy peered up to see the school principal herself pushing through the throng of kids. "What's the meaning of this? Did you need to go to the bathroom? You're old enough to go by yourself, aren't you?"

"Leave my sister alone!" came Lacy's voice, and Tracy felt the relief wash over her when she saw her twin sister stand in front of her, hands on her chubby little hips, defiantly looking up at the principal. Tracy could feel Lacy's cat snarling and hissing inside her, and for a moment she wondered if their two twin bobcats would just burst forth and shut everyone's mouths for good. "I said leave her alone!"

"Shame, shame, shame!" chanted the kids.

"Tracy's gonna pee on the playground!" someone squealed.

"Tracy's gonna take a leak on the lawn!" someone else howled.

"Tracy doesn't know how to go to the bathroom!"

"Shame! Shame! Shame!"

Tracy hugged herself on the ground, tears streaming down her face as her sister stood over her protectively. But Lacy was just a kid too, and Tracy could feel her older twin beginning to lose her nerve, lose her temper, just straight up lose it!

A moment later Tracy felt herself say screw it, and then both sisters' animals burst forth in a blur of movement! The two young bobcats leapt up at the school principal, their tiny claws out, their sharp little teeth bared. Tracy heard the principal scream, and she wondered if her cat was going to kill the woman! But then she realized that she had more control over her animal than she'd thought, and she laughed in delight when she and her sister landed on all fours and looked up at their handiwork.

"Shame, shame, shame!" squealed Lacy through

her bobcat, and Tracy squealed too when she saw that the principal was standing there in a state of shock, gasping, hyperventilating, panting, sobbing . . . and completely naked, her clothes lying in tatters and shreds around her trembling feet!

"Do you need to go to the bathroom?" Tracy asked as the kids began to scream. "Aren't you old enough to go by yourself?

"Shame, shame, shame!" hissed Lacy, bouncing up and down on all fours as the schoolyard descended into absolute chaos.

And then the principal fainted, collapsing on the soft playground with a little sigh, her eyes rolling up in her head, her mouth twisting into something that looked like a delirious smile.

"We should probably go, sis," whispered Lacy, sniffing the principal as if to make sure she was alive. "I don't think school is gonna work out for us."

6

<u>THIRTY YEARS EARLIER</u>
<u>CAMBRIDGE, ENGLAND</u>

Everett blinked himself back into focus as the gasps and giggles rose from the audience of college students who'd been bored out of their minds thus far—until they'd looked up and seen that their teacher—a handsome young graduate student—was now standing naked before them like one of those Greek Gods from the mythology he'd been droning on about.

"Bloody hell," Everett grunted, scratching his thick long hair as he looked down past his long cock and heavy balls, down at the torn clothes lying by his feet. He loved saying "Bloody hell." It made him feel more British, and he'd always liked the authority projected by his stately accent. Of course, he knew full well that a British accent only sounded authoritative because the damned Brits had colonized a good chunk of the world, including America and India, which were now two of the three largest countries on the globe. He shouldn't be celebrating that. Shouldn't be perpetuating that history.

Besides, saying "Bloody hell" right now was the understatement of the century, Everett thought, frowning as he tried to remember what had happened. A part of him suggested that perhaps he might think of covering his crotch, hiding his shame from the twenty-year olds who were staring wide eyed as if they weren't sure this was really happening.

Everett stood there in silence for a long moment before he realized that he must have Changed to his Tiger and Changed back almost instantaneously! A flash-Change, if you will! Had his students even seen the tiger? Perhaps it had happened so fast it hadn't registered! After all, no one was screaming or running. In fact, everyone was . . . was . . . clapping! Clapping and cheering!

Everett broke into a wide smile as he placed his hands on his hips and then shrugged as his students gave him a standing ovation, whooping and whistling like this was the goddamned circus and he was the feature act! Or the feature freak!

"Thank you," he said in his regal accent, which sounded perfectly appropriate as he strolled past his lecture-podium and turned so everyone could see his muscular arse. He knew he'd just lost his place as a PhD student, and he was probably going to be arrested. And shouldn't he feel ashamed?! Wasn't there even a shred of shame in him?! Nope—though he did feel oddly guilty about *not* feeling shame!

"Stay in school, chaps," he said with a grin as he finished his twirl just as the classroom door burst open and three security guards rushed in. "I need to run."

Then with another shrug of his muscular shoulders, Everett let his tiger burst forth. A moment later he'd crashed through the window of the ground-floor classroom, racing across the manicured lawns with blinding speed, disappearing into the English countryside.

7

Everything seemed to disappear for a moment, and Tracy screamed as she felt herself being pulled into what seemed like nothingness. Then suddenly she could see, and she realized she was back inside the dragon!

"Everett!" she screamed, turning around and around as she looked for her mate. She was in human form again, naked again, and she screamed again as that memory of her childhood shame

came roaring back like it had grown more powerful over the years. She couldn't understand why
that memory had popped up again. She couldn't
understand why it was having such an impact on
her. Yeah, at the time it had been kinda traumat-
ic. But it had also been fun, hadn't it? She and
her sister had disappeared into the mountains
of Colorado, living as bobcats, hunting for food,
roaming the hills like free animals. There'd been
some news articles about what had happened in
the schoolyard, but it had sounded too fantastic
and hokey to be taken seriously. Some kids swear-
ing they saw two girls turn into cats? A teacher
who couldn't be sure what had happened?

And what *had* happened, Tracy asked herself as
she forced herself to calm down. She was alone
in this dragon's belly, and somehow she knew
that she'd been pulled back here because of that
childhood memory. She was alone here, and her
mate was alone somewhere else. Was he still in
that dark pit of hell? Back in the beautiful land-
scape of heaven? Was the dragon's belly some
kind of in-between space? Purgatory? Was *any* of
this real?! Was *she* even real?

"Lacy," she whispered, sinking down to her
knees as she felt a deep yearning to talk to her
sister. There was too much going on. She needed

her twin. She needed that part of herself back. "Lacy, where are you? I need you. I can't do this alone. Lacy! Lacy! *Lacy*!"

8

Lacy! Lacy! Lacy!

Lacy saw the words spinning through the universe like they were physical objects, and she squealed in delight as she and Darius spun through space and time like it was an amusement park ride! She could see the bond between her and her mate like it was a golden rope tethering the two of them together, her and her lion, the King and Queen of the jungle!

She sighed as she twisted and turned, feeling herself smile wide as she looked over at Darius. Somehow she could see the man and the lion all at once, and although that was impossible in the world of flesh and blood, in the world of spirit it somehow made perfect sense!

"This is awesome!" she squealed, spinning around like a snowflake, that golden rope connecting her to her mate like an indestructible anchor. She looked below her, gasping when she saw John Benson's office in Abu Dhabi, saw her own body on the floor, her mate's body holding her in death. Her friends were gathered around, frozen in the image like it was a painting. The image was still like a snapshot, but somehow it was full of life, and Lacy realized she could *see* the emotions of every person in that room! There was fear, horror, and grief. But there was also faith, hope, and gratitude! Those other Shifters understood that Lacy and Darius could never die, were travelers through space and time, able to traverse Light and Dark by virtue of their fated bond.

She could see Magda the Witch, her eyes narrowed in concentration. The witch was trying to use her magic to reach out to Lacy and Darius. She was seeking the power to bring them back to the world of flesh and blood, and Lacy sighed again when she saw it so clearly: Magda was connected to magic that came from Light and sorcery that came from Darkness. The two sides were flowing through her like rivers, but the rivers were raging, in disharmony, sometimes the Light rising, sometimes the Dark flooding through.

"Are you seeing this?" Darius asked as the two of them floated above the scene. "Can you see our Shifter friends? Lacy, I can see the animal and the human in each of them at once! It's . . . it's crazy! Do you see that too?"

Lacy nodded. "Yes. And I can see how every Shifter in the room is connected to both Light and Darkness: Their human connected to the Light, the animal to the Darkness! It's so beautiful!"

"So are you," Darius growled, turning to her, the lion and the man looking at her in a way that sent cosmic ripples through her bobcat and her woman and every other part of her spirit! "Come here, woman. You need to be taught a lesson for attempting to leave me."

Lacy squealed as the two of them whirled away from that scene of their seemingly dead bodies. She whizzed through space—or whatever this was—with a quickness that was exhilarating, feeling her lion chase after her like they were animals at play. In that moment she understood that it was all a big game, a big play, that they were all actors on the universe's stage, playing their roles as the universe played with them.

But then the thought scared her, because as she found herself being lost to a kind of joy she'd never believed was possible, it occurred to her that she and Darius could spend all of eternity together here and not even know it. Anything was possible here! She could feel her body and her spirit in perfect balance! She knew they could make love if they wanted! They could roam forests together if they wanted! They could do anything they wanted! Why go back?! The others would find their way to this afterlife paradise too, wouldn't they?!

But then Lacy looked down at herself and gasped when she saw that her belly was glowing with the same golden light that connected her to Darius. And suddenly she remembered that she was pregnant! She moaned out loud when she realized she could see her litter of kittens forming inside her. It was like a hologram of what they would be, even though they were barely zygotes at this point.

"We can't stay here," she gasped out loud, knowing that Darius had been thinking the same thing as they marveled at the splendor of the larger universe which was now their playground. "Darius, if we aren't back in the world of flesh and blood in time, we'll lose . . . lose everything!"

But Darius was looking off into the distance, and Lacy frowned as she tried to see what he was seeing. It took her a moment, but then she saw it: It was Everett the Tiger Shifter, and he was alone, in tiger form, roaring out loud as he twisted and turned, clawing at the air, snapping his massive jaws. It looked like he was fighting some invisible demons, and she blinked when she felt Darius being drawn towards his friend.

Lacy looked down at the golden thread that connected her with her mate. It was shining even brighter than before, and she felt a calmness flow through her when she reminded herself that nothing could break this bond. They were mated, and they couldn't be split apart. They'd come here for a purpose. They were on a mission. They were King and Queen of the jungle, and they were responsible for their roles in this great game the universe was playing.

She thought back to the other couples of what was now her crew: Adam the Dragon and Ash his mate; Bart the Bear and Bismeeta the Leopard; Caleb the Wolf and Magda the Fox. As she blinked she could see all the connections laid out before her like a map:

Adam's father Murad: The Black Dragon driven insane because he killed his mate!

Bart and Ash's parents, Bear Shifters who'd killed other Shifters in some misguided attempt to "cure" them!

Caleb the Wolf, who'd been plagued by the guilt of killing his own father.

Magda the Witch, who'd given herself to Dark Magic and was now facing the challenge of balancing her two sources of power!

"There's someone missing," Lacy muttered as she recalled that last conversation in John Benson's office, when he'd explained to them that the only way Magda could harness enough power to stop Murad was by drawing on the combined strength of their crew—their crew of mated Shifters. Shifters who'd created that indestructible bond by finding their fated mates. Shifters who'd found strength and balance in each other and could use that magical bond to bring balance back to a lopsided world! "One missing couple," she whispered again as she saw how Darius was once again being drawn towards the Tiger Shifter.

And then she heard it again.

Or rather, she *saw* it.

Lacy! Lacy! Lacy!

The wordsn came through again, and it was more than sound, it was more than sight, it was more than anything she could understand. But then she understood.

It was love.

Multidimensional love.

The fabric of the universe.

The only thing that was real.

The only thing worth fighting for.

The only thing worth dying for.

In an instant Lacy was flooded with sensations of such overwhelming love that she screamed in ecstasy. She could see all the love surrounding her and Darius, and she understood that everything they'd done, everything they *were*, was defined by love.

The love between fated mates.

The love between members of a crew.

The love between sisters.

And as that ecstasy of pure love flowed through her spirit, Lacy turned to her mate and smiled and nodded.

"Go to your friend," she whispered to Darius, looking down at the golden rope of their fated bond. "Then come find me."

Darius whipped his head around, and Lacy saw his lion's eyes blaze with a yearning to go with her. But then Darius nodded, looking down at their cosmic bond and turning once again to that vision of Everett the Tiger.

And then *poof*, they were gone.

9

"**P**oof!" said the female figure bathed in golden light—light so bright that Tracy had to shield her eyes. It took her a moment to recognize the voice, and when she opened her eyes again she saw what had to be an hallucination, a vision, a mirage of the mind.

"Of course it's a mirage!" Tracy said, snorting

out loud as she saw her sister's familiar curvy shape standing before her in a dragon's belly. "Poof to you too! Shoo! You aren't real!"

"What do you mean, I'm not real?!" said Lacy, hands on her hips. "I travel through space and time for you, and this is the welcome I get?! You always were a spoiled brat, and this confirms it!"

"Spoiled?! Spoiled by whom? You?" Tracy shouted, smiling wide as she decided that to hell with it, she might as well have a conversation with a mirage! "Hah!"

"Spoiled by *everyone*!" said Lacy, hands still on her hips, body still bathed in golden light. "The baby bobcat of the family!"

"What family?" said Tracy. "We barely even knew our parents!"

"*This* family!" said Lacy, holding her arms out wide. "Come here, sis. Come here."

Tracy felt her arms open too as she staggered toward her sister and gave her a hug, frowning when she realized that she had clothes on again— clothes that felt strangely familiar. She backed away from the hug and looked down at herself.

"Um, why am I wearing this T-shirt from like thirty years ago?" she said, blinking down at the old *Backstreet Boys* t-shirt that she could've sworn had been ripped to shreds decades earlier. "And how is it I can feel my body again? What's happening, sis? Where am I? *What* am I?"

Lacy sighed and shook her head. "You're dead, hon. We both are. But just kinda dead. Not forever-dead. Just until . . ." She shook her head again, waving her hands about like she wanted to start over with the explanation. "Listen, Tracy," she said finally, a grave seriousness coming over her round face, "before you died, did you and Everett get to . . . um . . . you know . . . *bond*?"

"We kissed," said Tracy. "Just one kiss. Maybe two. Nothing more."

Lacy looked like she was about to burst into tears, but then she forced a smile. "Was Everett here with you? Have you seen him since you—"

"We died together," said Tracy, feeling a strange glow light her from the inside—the same kind of glow that was shining from Lacy. Not as bright, though. "We're mates, sis. We're connected. Even that one kiss bonded us, though maybe not completely." She cocked her head and frowned as a quizzical smile broke on her face. "Not as completely as you and the lion, looks like! What's his name?"

"Darius," said Lacy, placing her hands on her

belly in a way that Tracy couldn't ignore. "He's with Everett the Tiger right now."

"Doing what?" said Tracy. "And what are *you* doing here? Oh, no! Did you two get killed by the Black Dragon, just like Everett and I?"

"Wait, what? Murad killed you?"

"No, not *that* Black Dragon!" said Tracy. She waved her arms above her head and then turned on her feet, pointing at the dark walls of living, breathing, dragon-flesh. "*This* Black Dragon!"

Lacy frowned, looking around her like she was only just noticing that they were inside a sea-beast's big fat belly. "Ohmygod," she whispered. "Murad's mate? She's . . . she's already here? Already emerged? Tracy, we have to kill it! We have to destroy it before—"

But the Black she-Dragon let out that screeching wail that threatened to shatter both sisters' eardrums even in this weird reality, and Lacy gasped as she looked around once more at their cage.

"Oh, yeah," said Tracy with a half-grin. "Shoulda warned you: Don't mention M-U-R-A-D out loud or else—"

But again the dragon let out that mournful cry, turning its body and diving deeper into the dark ocean. Both sisters were tossed around like ping-pong balls until the dragon settled back down, but by then they were both giggling.

"I guess the dragon can spell," said Tracy, taking a strange delight in the surprise on her twin's face. "Also, perhaps we shouldn't talk about killing her, considering we're inside her belly right now. Kinda at her mercy."

Lacy looked more confused than ever, and Tracy just sighed and took a breath. Then she told her everything: What had happened on the beach; what Murad's mate had said to them about going to the Light and finding the human woman who'd been killed; about how there was hope this beast could reunite with its human, perhaps reunite with Murad, which might somehow . . .

" . . . somehow bring *both* Black Dragons back into balance," Lacy said softly, her voice shaking with excitement. "That just might work, Tracy!"

"But how do we find a human woman who's been killed decades ago?" said Tracy. "This beast said something about how mated Shifters can travel between Light and Darkness, that the human is somewhere in the Light. What is that? Heaven?"

Lacy shook her head. "There's no heaven. You know that."

Tracy exhaled slowly, thinking back to what

she and Everett had seen and felt before getting pulled down to the Darkness. "I . . . I *don't* know that, Lacy. I think there *is* a heaven. I think I saw it. I think I was in it. With Everett! I saw beautiful rocky mountains, and he saw wide open grasslands. It was like our personal heavens, but we were in it together! I don't know how to explain it, but it felt so . . . so *real*!"

Lacy shook her head, pity showing on her face—pity that annoyed Tracy. "Then why are you here, inside a dragon's belly? Why isn't Everett here with you? If you and Everett found heaven, then we'd be having this conversation in the mountains, maybe with a bottle of heavenly tequila sitting on a flat rock near our big butts."

Tracy closed her eyes, feeling that sensation of shame rolling back through her. It puzzled her, like the feeling was coming from somewhere deep inside. Again that memory of the schoolyard incident came back to her, but the shame went beyond that, was deeper than that, older than that.

"The schoolyard incident?" Lacy said, her eyes going wide as she snorted. "You remember that? Oh God, that was so funny!"

"How do you know I was thinking of that?" Tracy said. "Can you like,*see* my thoughts? And why *wouldn't* I remember that? We're the same age, sis. We're *twins*!"

Again that look of pity flashed on Lacy's face, and now Tracy thought she could see directly into her sister's mind, her memories, her past. A past that was different from her own. How could it be different?! They were twins! Born on the same day! Right? Right?!

"Right?!" Tracy whispered, finishing her thoughts in words, even though it seemed like there was no difference between thoughts and words, past and present, reality and illusion. "What aren't you telling me, sis?"

"Something I didn't even know I knew," whispered Lacy, shaking her head and looking away. She looked back at Tracy, reaching out and touching her hair. "Tracy, do you remember your parents?"

"What do you mean *my* parents? We have the same parents, Lacy!"

Lacy shook her head, squinting as if she was looking at something, looking at the past itself. "No," she whispered. "Our parents—the couple you remember from our early years—weren't Shifters." She paused and took a breath. "And neither was I. Not until you Turned me."

Tracy staggered back, bumping up against the pulsating walls of the dragon's belly. She could tell that the dragon was listening to everything, soaking it all in as it glided deep beneath the ocean—or perhaps through the clouds—it was all the same in this messed up reality.

"A few days after I was born, my father found you in the mountains, naked and screaming," said Lacy, her eyelids fluttering as if she was seeing all of this in her mind's eye. "He couldn't leave you there to die, so he brought you home."

"And decided to just *keep* me? No calling the police? No checking for reports of a missing child?"

Lacy sighed, squinting as if she was seeing all of this on some cosmic screen. "No," she whispered. "He said it was a sign from God. A test of some kind. Like Baby Moses being abandoned and set adrift. He thought he was meant to find the child and raise it as his own! Raise *you*as his own!"

Suddenly Tracy could see it, see it all, see them all! She gasped as the vision enveloped them, vivid images of what had happened back then:

"This is a child of sin, not God!" came her mother's voice, high-pitched with accusation. "You fathered a child out of wedlock, and you bring her into my house with some story of finding her in the woods?! Shame on you! *Shame!*"

"How can you accuse me of being anything but true to you, true to God?!" snarled her father as the two girl babies gurgled and giggled, staring up as if they were amused by what was unfolding. "How can you doubt the task presented to us by God? Shame on you! *Shame!*"

Tracy watched the vision as the argument escalated, the accusations flying back and forth like daggers, doubt and fear ripping through the married couple like it was coming from somewhere outside them. Tracy could see herself and her sister, the two babies surprisingly calm, both of them still gurgling. They looked like two peas in a pod, like they were meant to be together, like there was a strand of fate connecting them.

"Lacy, look," said Tracy softly as she watched the two babies reach out and hold hands even though it seemed impossible for newborns to have that kind of control. "Ohmygod, look!"

Lacy nodded beside her, and as the two sisters watched in awed silence, Baby Tracy Changed.

She Changed into a bobcat kitten, soft golden fur, sharp white teeth, eyes focused and blazing.

She Changed, and she bit her sister.

"I . . . I Turned you," Tracy whispered in shock as she watched her father and mother leap back in fear, crossing themselves and muttering prayers as if the devil himself had just showed up.

Time flashed forward in their shared vision, and Tracy felt raw emotions of such depth pass through her that she felt like she was nothing *but* emotion! She watched as her parents dragged her away from her sister, her father tossing the mewling kitten across the room and then jumping back in fear as the mother furiously dabbed at Lacy's wound.

But Lacy wasn't crying, and Tracy swore she could *see* the Turning happening, Shifter blood entering Lacy's veins, moving up to her heart, getting pumped back throughout her body. Tracy wasn't sure if it had really happened that fast or if time was just being sped up in their vision. Perhaps the vision was years compressed down to minutes. She couldn't tell, but it didn't really matter. It was a true vision. The feelings were so deep that it couldn't *not* be true. If this was just an illusion, then *everything* in the universe was an illusion too.

Tracy's head spun as the vision sped up, its in-

tensity rising as her parents screamed, Baby Tracy snarled and , little Lacy giggled as her wound
slowly closed up like it was a medical miracle.

"What the hell?" Lacy muttered, and Tracy nodded in dumbstruck agreement as they watched
their father go down on his knees and begin to
sob like he'd lost his mind.

"It's my fault!" he howled, holding his arms
out, palms upturned like he was begging for for-
giveness. "I did it! I betrayed my wife! Betrayed
my God! Betrayed myself! This abomination of
a child is mine! This inhuman creature, this demon, this monster . . . I created her with my sin!"

The two sisters stared at the vision of their
blubbering father confessing his sins. They
watched with wide eyes as he talked of meeting
an alluring woman in the mountains, naked and
wild, with eyes like a cat, hair like golden fur, long,
beautiful nails like claws. She'd been in heat, and
he'd given in to temptation, pouring his seed into
her out in the wild even as guilt and shame filled
his own body.

He went on and on, revealing that she'd showed
up months later with the child, her once-beauti-
ful body shriveled and racked, like she was dying
of something unnamable.

"You are not my fated mate," she'd whispered to him. "And I now have to pay the price for taking your seed. Do what you will with the child."

"Oh, my God," Tracy whispered as she gazed upon the image of her real mother, a cat Shifter who was clearly dying. "What's happening? Did I do that? Did I kill my own mother by just . . . just being *born*?!"

"We both did," came Lacy's voice, and Tracy blinked as she realized that she and her sister were holding hands as they watched their past reveal itself in the dragon's belly. "Look. Over there. To our left."

Tracy frowned as she turned to the simultaneous vision of her father on his knees. Her attention moved on to Lacy's real mother—the human woman. Tracy felt a chill go through her when she saw that the woman had stopped her accusations and hysterics and was . . . was *smiling*!

But it wasn't a smile of pleasure or satisfaction. It was a smile that oozed relief, resignation, a dismal acceptance of fate, submission to the consequences of their choices.

"Stand up, my husband," she whispered, her lips trembling through that thin smile. "Stand beside me, for we are both sinners."

Their father shook his head, unable to meet his wife's gaze. "You have committed no sin other than the sin of trusting your husband." He shook his head again, his shoulders slumping in despair. "Your husband who lay with an animal! Seduced by the devil in disguise! I can never stand beside you again!"

"Then I will kneel beside you in shame," said his wife, going down to the floor and crawling toward her husband. "Because I have layed with an animal too," she whispered, glancing over at Baby Lacy and then at her husband. "And the child that emerged from my womb is *his* spawn, not yours."

Tracy and Lacy stared in shock as the two babies in their vision giggled again, holding hands like they were kindred souls. And then Tracy realized that the wound on Baby Lacy was completely healed. Not even a scar remained!

"Ohmygod, Lacy," she whispered. "I didn't Turn you with that bite! You were already a Shifter! That was just my animal playing with its sister!"

Lacy's lips were moving but she wasn't saying a word. She just stared at that vision, her eyes finally rolling up in her head as if she was going to faint right there in the dragon's belly.

"Oh, God, you're right," she gurgled, almost

choking as the realization hit both sisters at once even as they watched their parents sob and hug each other in that vision.

The vision was still going, but Tracy could no longer hear what her father and his wife were saying to each other. She could feel their emotions, though. Dark emotions. Shame and guilt, self-loathing and fear, darkness and no light. No light at all.

"No," Lacy whispered, her grip on Tracy's hand tightening. "Please, no! I can't watch this!"

But they both continued to watch as their father reached behind a bookshelf and pulled out his shotgun, loading and cocking it as his wife crossed herself and muttered something under her breath. Their father went back down on his knees, drawing his wife close to him, placing his head directly beneath hers, lodging the double barrels of the weapon firmly beneath his chin.

Then he pulled the trigger, and the vision exploded into nothingness, into darkness, pure black so deep and all-encompassing that it almost made Tracy choke.

The darkness seemed like it would consume them both, and Tracy wondered if they were getting pulled to that pit of Darkness again. She held her sister's hand tight as she tried to see through the wall of black. She could still feel the remnants of their parents' emotions, but at the same time she was feeling strangely liberated, oddly excited, like this revelation had opened up a doorway of sorts, freed them from something that was holding them back, pushing them towards some broader part of their destiny.

"Finally," came a female voice through the darkness, and Tracy gasped. It was her real mother's voice, even though she couldn't possibly remember her mother's voice. Still, she knew it was. She just knew.

"Yes, took you two long enough," came a male voice, and then Tracy saw the silhouettes of the two bobcat Shifters slowly take shape until she could see them clearly.

Instantly she knew these two were brother and sister! Bobcat siblings! The man was Lacy's father! The woman was Tracy's mother!

"Holy Mother of God," Tracy whispered in awe, feeling her face light up in a smile when she realized that this wasn't a vision. This was freakin' real. Well, as real as anything could be in an undersea dragon's belly!

"Um, I prefer just Mom," said the woman, smiling at Tracy with her eyes—the eyes of a cat.

"And you can call me Father," said the man,

glancing at Lacy and shrugging. "Or Dad, if you want."

"Um, nice to meet you, I suppose," Lacy stammered. She glanced over at Tracy, blinking in astonishment. "Is this real?" she whispered.

Tracy snorted, hands on her hips as she stared at her older sister—who was neither older nor a sister—but hey, old habits died hard. "I was about to ask you the same thing, moron," she whispered back.

"So we're . . . we're cousins?" Lacy said, shaking her head and blinking five times as if to make sure she wasn't hallucinating. She turned back to the two bobcat Shifters. "You two are brother and sister? Bobcat Shifters who took human mates just so you could . . . what, produce offspring?"

The woman—Tracy's mother—took a long breath, her eyes filling with tears that shone like diamonds in the dark. "The needs of our animals are strong, fierce, undeniable," she said softly. "There is a drive to seek out our fated mates, but we lost hope of ever finding them. Not every Shifter finds its fated mate, you know. We believed we were the last of our kind, and the needs of our animals to produce young were too great. And so we did what we did."

"What you did was destroy a marriage, destroy two human lives!" Lacy said, her eyes burning with the anger of her cat.

"Yes," said Lacy's father, his slender frame shaking as he looked away from his daughter's accusing glare. When he looked back up, his eyes were shining with tears too. "And we paid the price. Paid it with our lives."

"And we are still paying the price in the afterlife," said Tracy's mother. "We will be paying the price for all eternity. Those are the consequences of mating with someone who is not your fated mate."

"So then what kind of creatures are we?" said Tracy, feeling the same indignation roll through her. "The offspring of an unnatural coupling? Some kind of monsters?!"

The female bobcat laughed, and the dragon let out a low wail just then, as if to remind them of where what were. "We are all monsters, my dear child," said the woman. "We will never be part of the human world, human society, human civilization." She reached out and touched the walls of the dragon's insides, sending a shiver through the beast like it could feel her touch. "This monster knows that, and so does her mate Murad. When this beast materializes fully in the world of flesh and blood, crawls out of the Darkness and into the real world, we will all experience a new beginning, a fresh start, a clean slate."

Tracy stared at her mother, then at her uncle, finally back at her cousin-sister Lacy. "They're insane," she whispered. "Our parents are nutcases, Lacy! All four of them were nutcases—even the human ones! We can't listen to any of this crap! There's hope for the world! There is Light in this dragon! I know it! We just have to reunite the dragon with the human woman! We can do it, Lacy! We can go to the Light and bring back that human soul!"

Lacy nodded slowly, her fierce gaze focused on the two Shifters standing before her. "What happened when you two died?" she asked softly. "I know that when an unmated Shifter dies, its human and animal gets split. The human goes to the Light, and the animal goes to the Darkness."

Tracy frowned as she listened. "But the two of you aren't unmated. Both of you did mate— just not with your fated partners. So yeah, Lacy's right. What happened when you died?"

"The most wonderful thing," said the female bobcat, her eyes shining with a darkness that made Tracy shudder.

"We didn't lose our animals to the Darkness at all!" said the male bobcat, his tight, catlike face broadening to a grin that showed teeth that were yellowed and chipped, with jagged edges like he'd been chewing on rocks or grinding his canines against each other for eternity!

"We went *with* our animals to the Darkness," whispered her mother, hissing out loud like a bobcat gone mad.

"We live in the Darkness as humans!" said Lacy's father, rubbing his hands together . . . hands that were covered in clawmarks, like he'd been clawing at himself for years. "We are powerful! Immortal in the flesh! Able to do what we please!"

"With *whomover* we please!" giggled Tracy's mother, her tone exuding a dark sexual energy that made Tracy want to scream and cover her eyes, her mouth, her ears . . . block out all her senses!

"Ohmygod, it's the choice you made as humans," whispered Lacy, backing away from the giggling Shifters and pulling Tracy back with her. "The choice to give in to your animal lust and mate outside of the fated bond. It was a human choice to give in to the animal's needs, and now your humans are lost to the Darkness too!"

"We are not lost," said her father. "We are *found*!"

"And now we've found you!" said Tracy's mother with a happy smile that made Tracy clutch Lacy's arm in fear. "Come with us! We're family! We can be a family forever! Through time and space!"

"The Darkness is beautiful once you get to know it," said the male bobcat through his yellowed teeth. "There are others like us there. Thousands to choose from. Pleasures of the flesh that you can't even imagine!"

"We aren't like you," whispered Lacy, pulling Tracy close and pointing at their crazy-as-fuck parents. "We never lost hope. We waited for our fated mates and we found them."

"Yes, you found them. But then you lost them," said the female bobcat with a shrug. She spread her arms out wide and twirled around like a lunatic, leaning her head back and laughing out loud. "Where are your fated mates? They are gone, my little ones! Gone because of the choices you made! You *are* just like us!"

"What the hell is she talking about, Lacy? What choices?"

"Dark choices," whispered the male bobcat.

"Suicide," said the female bobcat, still twirling, still laughing. Then she stopped and pointed at

Lacy's belly. "And gambling with the life of your unborn child! Shame! Shame! Shame!"

"Shame! Shame! Shame!" hissed the male bobcat, pretending to rock an invisible baby as Tracy turned to her cousin in horror.

She could see that Lacy was losing her nerve, losing her calm, losing control. Her eyelids were fluttering, and Tracy watched as Lacy's white eyeballs began to cloud over with black, as if she was being lost to the Darkness!

"Lacy, no! There's no shame in what you did! You did it for me! Because you loved me! Don't listen to them! Lacy! Lacy! *Lacy!*"

But Lacy was fading to black before her very eyes, and Tracy knew she had to make a decision.

The same decision Lacy had made for her.

"You followed me into death," she whispered to her fading sister—and Lacy *was* her sister, family technicalities be damned. "And I'm going to follow you into Darkness."

Tracy took one last look at the two dark bobcats who were their parents, and she smiled and closed her eyes, reaching for those old feelings of shame that she knew lived inside her too. Feelings that would open up a path to the Darkness just like it was doing for Lacy.

But she wasn't scared, because even as she felt

herself being consumed by the Darkness, she felt a part of her reach back to that one kiss on the beach, that kiss with her fated mate. Would that one kiss be enough for her tiger to blaze a path across the universe to find her? To bring her back?

"Everett," she whispered as she floated away into dark nothingness, smiling as the words of an old poem came back to her even though she didn't remember ever reading it:

Tiger, Tiger, burning bright,
In the forests of the night.
One beautiful kiss.
One true mate.
One chance in hell.

10

"**I**'m in hell," muttered Everett, whirling around in the Darkness surrounding him. He was in tiger form, snarling and snapping at the ethereal beasts that were wailing and howling around him in this dark pit.

He looked up to see if those damned Bear Shifters were still looking down at him. He could make out their shadowy figures, but they weren't stand-ing there with hands on their furry haunches like before. No, they were standing at the edge of the pit, up on their hind legs, massive paws swinging as they fought back thousands upon thousands of beasts that were leaping up in a wild effort to crawl out of the dark pit, out through the gateway, out of hell and into the world of flesh and blood!

"Yup," he said again. "I'm in hell."

"Correction," came a familiar voice from his left. "*We're* in hell, brother."

"Darius!" roared Everett, picking up the scent of the Lion Shifter before he actually saw him. It took a moment for his image to materialize, but when it did, Everett roared again, this time in awe.

Because Darius was glowing with a beautiful golden light, his lion's fur shimmering with en-ergy that seemed on par with the sun! His eyes were clear and focused, and from the edge of the glow that enveloped him was a strand of golden light that Everett immediately understood con-nected Darius to his mate! His fated mate! His bonded mate!

Everett whipped his tiger's head around, des-perately hoping that he'd see the same golden thread linking him to his own fated mate. But his heart dropped like a stone when he didn't see a thing. Then he realized Tracy was no longer there, and he roared as a terrible fear whipped through him! He was supposed to protect her! But now she was gone! When had that happened? *How* had that happened?!

"Relax, bud," said the lion, coming close, his presence calming down Everett's tiger. "She's with her sister. She's safe."

"How can either of our mates be safe when the two of us aren't with them?" growled Everett. "It's our job to protect our mates, remember? Or do you not give a damn now that you're the Golden King of the Cosmic Jungle?! Got bigger responsibilities now that you're some kind of Angel of Light?"

Darius chuckled, the sound coming out as a deep rumble. "Actually, yes. We *both* have bigger responsibilities. All four of us do, in fact. But first you've got to get your head straight, brother."

"Easy for you to say," snapped Everett, once again looking around in search of his mate, his tiger's head again twisting to see if that cosmic thread had magically appeared. If it did, maybe he could just pull Tracy back to him! "You're connected to your fated mate. You can never lose her. But that goddamn she-dragon took me before I could complete my bond with my mate! You want help me get my head straight, then help me find my mate!"

"You can only find her by looking within yourself now, brother," said Darius, his calmness almost sending Everett into a murderous rage!

"What the hell does that mean? When did you turn into some kind of mystical sage?! Here, give me that! I'll pull *both* our mates back to us!" Everett leapt toward Darius, his tiger's paws reaching for that golden thread of Light that connected the lion to his bobcat mate.

But his paws just passed through the golden thread, and Everett roared in anguish as he whirled around helplessly one more time. Above him he could still see and hear those Bear Shifters beating back those soulless animals. His mate was missing. And Darius was standing in front of him, happily bathed in golden light, connected forever to his mate, speaking words of annoyingly hokey wisdom.

"There's a reason the two of you got separated," Darius said. "There's something each of you has to come to terms with about yourselves before you can complete your bond. That's the path fate takes. That's the way destiny works. The universe brought the two of you together, and so if it split you apart, it's because there's some part of your private, individual journey that has to be completed before you can complete your fated bond. Some task to be completed. Some part of yourself that needs to be understood, needs to be accepted. Lacy is helping your mate with her task. And looks like it's my job to help you with yours, brother."

Everett wanted to snap back at the annoyingly pompous lion, but something about Darius's words hit home. What had Everett told Tracy when they were swallowed whole by a sea-dragon? Hadn't he said it reminded him of Jonah and the Whale? How did that story end? It only ended when Jonah accepted that he was chosen to do something, and he could never hide from his responsibility. And to finish his task, Jonah had to understand himself, accept himself, believe that he was worthy of his mission!

"All right," Everett finally snarled, his tiger's tail moving from side to side as he faced his friend the lion. "Where do we start, O Great Wise Lion of the Light?"

Darius raised a golden eyebrow and then shrugged his lion's shoulders. "Beats me. I guess maybe we start with your parents? How was your relationship with them?"

Everett convulsed with laughter, his blazing tiger's eyes going wide as he stared at his friend. "Are you serious? *You're* going to be my goddamn psychiatrist?! Did you even finish high-school before joining the circus?"

"I probably learned more about life in the circus than you did in your ivory tower of academia," Darius shot back. "Oh, wait, you didn't actually get your PhD, did you?"

Everett stopped laughing. "How do you know that?" he growled.

Darius squinted, his gaze focused just above Everett's head. "I can . . . I can *see* it, Everett! I see your . . . your *shame*!"

Everett snorted. "Now I know for sure that you're full of it. I've never felt a moment of shame in my entire life!"

"And that's why you're ashamed!" Darius said. "I see it, Everett! Your parents! They were both highly intellectual, logical-minded Tiger Shifters. They believed that the animal parts of themselves brought them down, debased them, made them less than human. That's how they raised you! That's what they taught you! But in your heart of hearts you understood that your tiger made you *more* than human, not less! That messed you up, brother! The conflict between wanting to believe what your parents told you and needing to believe what your instincts were telling you!"

Everett stared in muted shock at his buddy, wondering if the lion really had turned into some kind of all-knowing magical shrink! What the hell?*How* the hell? Could Darius really see all that?! See his past? See what was inside him?

Everett looked around, and then he suddenly saw them: His parents, clear as day!

"Bloody hell," he growled, crouching down and baring his teeth at what he was sure was just a vision, a mirage, an hallucination. "You're dead. I watched both of you die!"

"Hear that, love?" said his father, raising an eyebrow and glancing at his mother. "He watched us die!"

"How sweet," said his mother, sighing and placing a hand on her heart—a hand that was covered in scars . . . scars from old clawmarks, like she'd been clawing at her own skin for years! "Isn't he sweet? Our baby boy!"

Everett felt a chill go through him as he looked into his parents' eyes and saw nothing but a void, nothing but darkness, nothing but death. They were both in human form, which puzzled Everett. Wasn't this the Darkness? A place for Shifters' animals only? After all, he was in tiger form, Darius was in lion form, and those damned bears were still all brown fur and snouts! Humans couldn't manifest here! Couldn't survive here! Couldn't *be* here!

"We aren't human," whispered his mother, her eyes blazing with the dark energy of her twisted tiger. "We're monsters."

"Monsters," growled his father, smiling wide and showing off teeth that were like fangs, yellowed and chipped, biting down on lips that were broken and bleeding, like they'd been bleeding for a hundred years! "Just like you. Come, join us at the dinner table! We'll read the newspaper together! You still like the comics? Garfield the Cat, right?"

Everett's tiger recoiled from his father's outstretched arm, growling as it prepared to attack its own parents—or whatever these creatures were! They weren't human, but they weren't animal either. They were something else. Something deeply unbalanced. Something darker than the

Darkness. It reminded him of those strange Shifters he'd seen back at the circus, in fact.

Everett blinked as he felt his tiger's vision bring forth a clarity that made him gasp. Suddenly he understood! He didn't know *how* he understood, but he did! He could see it in the way his mother and father were standing—close together but also separated! There was no thread linking them! No golden thread, no silver string, not even a gnarled rope that glowed with the dark energy of this place.

"You aren't fated mates!" Everett finally blurted out, the answer coming out in words even as the thought formed in his frazzled brain. "You're both Shifters, but not true mates! You lost faith in your fate! Gave up on your destiny! Mated outside of the fated bond! That's why you both died so early! You lost what made you special, changed your own fate somehow!"

His mother sighed again, placing that scarred hand over her heart once more. She looked at Everett's father and shook her head. "He always was an ungrateful wretch, wasn't he?"

"If we hadn't mated, you wouldn't have been born!" said his father, crossing his eyebrows and shaking a trembling finger at Everett.

"I would have been born to someone else,"

growled Everett, suddenly certain of his destiny, his fate. "I was born for my fated mate, not for you! You didn't give me life! I live for her! For Tracy! Our bond would have pulled me to her regardless of whose womb I emerged from, whose seed I arose from! You have no one to blame but your own impatience! Your own lack of faith!"

"Faith in what? The legend of fated mates?" shrieked his mother, her jaws opening wide to reveal a toothless cavern that stank of death, reeked of shame, oozed with self-hatred. "There's no such thing! We waited for decades . . . waited for nothing! We died to give you life!"

"And our reward is a life of pleasure down here," whispered his father, his eyes shining with a crazed darkness that made Everett want to cry. He'd grieved for his parents as he watched them wither away in the world of flesh and blood, the healing powers of their tigers seemingly lost. He hadn't understood why it was happening back then—especially since he'd seen how easily his own tiger healed after even the most devastating wounds from its youthful recklessness. But he understood it now. Understood it in a way he wished he didn't!

"Why!" he roared in anguish as he watched

his parents slowly turn from him and walk away into the Darkness. "Why did I need to see that? Why did I need to know that? Why, Darius?! Why the *fuck* did I need to see that?!"

"Because whether you knew it or not, you blamed yourself for their deaths," said Darius. "And now you know that they are responsible for their own choices. You saw it in a moment of divine insight, buddy. You saw that your soul exists for your fated mate. You are free from the hold your parents had on you. You carried their shame with you, whether you knew it or not. But you aren't like them, bro. You're like me! You controlled your need to mate until fate rewarded you with the true one,*your* true one!"

"Then where is she!" roared Everett, the dark emotions rising up in him from that encounter with the twisted souls of his parents. "Where is she, Darius?! If the whole point of this was for me to learn the truth about my parents, that they lost faith in the promise of true mates, in the promise of destiny, that they somehow reasoned their way into getting their animals to mate outside of the fated bond, that they're existing as humans in the Darkness, living some life of carnal pleasure without the balance of human love . . .

if that's supposed to release me from whatever baggage I've been carrying, free me to complete my bond with my fated mate, then where *is* my mate?! Where *is* my true love?! What good are my own choices if I've lost her?! I might as well have mated with every female grad-student who showed up at my office after sunset!"

Everett paused as he felt his tiger tense up even as he felt the human in him relax. A part of him knew that Darius was right. Everett *had*controlled his need to mate, his need to take a woman, his need to give in to the animal lust which sometimes drove him close to madness. He hadn't known what he was holding out for. It was just instinct. An instinct that didn't come from his tiger alone or his human alone. An instinct that came from the meeting place of his animal and his human. An instinct that came from a place of perfect balance—or perhaps the need to *find* perfect balance: A balance that could only come from his fated mate.

He blinked through his tiger's eyes as he felt a wave of relief pass through him. Then he looked up and gasped as he *saw* the emotions leave him like they were living, breathing things: Guilt,

shame, loneliness. Isolation, anguish, restlessness. He smiled and nodded, blowing air from his
tiger's maws like he was sending those feelings off
into the Darkness, where they belonged. Then he
turned to Darius, a big smile on his tiger's face.

But the smile left him the next moment.

"Darius," he whispered, his tiger once again
tensing up like it had before, like it knew something was wrong. "Darius . . ."

"What's happening," growled the lion, pacing
in restless fury, swinging its mighty maned head
from side to side as if it was caught in a trap.
"What's happening? Why do I feel like . . . like . .
. oh, God, Lacy! *Lacy!*"

Everett stared in disbelief as that golden thread
that he knew connected Darius to Lacy turned
dark . . . so dark it was shining black like oil in the
moonlight, twisting and turning like a serpent!
The thread was still there, still strong, still unbroken. But it was shining with a different light.
A light that glinted of darkness.

And then, as Everett watched, that thread tightened, and Lacy exploded into being, still in human form, her body spinning in the air like she'd
been sucked up into a twister! She screamed as

she spun past the two big cats, and then her body disappeared into what looked like a hole within the dark pit where they stood, the same hole that Everett's parents had faded into!

That dark thread went taut, and a moment later Darius was pulled after his mate, his lion's strength useless against the infinite gravity of whatever force was pulling Lacy deeper into the Darkness.

"Darius!" Everett roared, trying to reach out and grab his buddy, grab both of them, pull them away! But he couldn't get to them. It was like he was being held back from that place of ultimate Darkness. "Darius, hold on! I'm coming!"

But Darius just roared, and as Everett watched in shock, the lion Changed back to the man, following his mate deeper into the Darkness.

"Bloody hell," Everett growled, stomping his feet as he realized that the only way he was going to be able to follow them into that place, that place where his own parents existed, was to re-possess those dark emotions that he'd just let go! Bring that guilt and shame back into him! Those emotions were the price of entry to this place! Lacy had somehow accessed her own darkest emotions, and she was being pulled into this pit of despair. Darius was being pulled down with her, thanks to the unbreakable bond between fated mates. What the hell was Everett supposed to do?! He wanted to go after his buddy, just like Darius had come for him. But what about Tracy?! Nothing was more important than his own mate!

And then he saw her come spinning onto the scene, and Everett just grinned like a madman. Somehow he understood exactly what was happening.

Tracy was going after her sister.

And Everett was going with her.

"Bloody hell," he whispered again, feeling his Change coming, feeling those dark emotions swirl up again in him as he reached out for his mate, preparing to take her hand and follow her into what might in fact*be* bloody hell . . .

11

"**B**loody hell," Tracy heard Everett say as she saw him reach for her, take her hand, and allow himself to be pulled to whatever place this was.

She landed on her feet with a thud. A hard thud that sent shooting pain throughout her body. She looked down, grimacing at how heavy she felt, how heavy the atmosphere felt. It was like gravity was doubled in this place, and she frowned as she heard three more thuds around her.

"Tracy! I'm here!" came Everett's voice, and relief washed through her when she saw her mate standing there, naked and human, his darkly handsome face twisted in a grimace as he stared at his own feet, lifting them one at a time and frowning. "Why do my feet feel so damned heavy?"

Tracy ran to Everett, throwing herself at him and almost knocking him over with her strangely exaggerated weight down in this place. He grunted as he caught her, smiling wide and leaning in close. "Got you," he said.

"Just about," she said, blinking as she looked down at their bodies squished together. Then she turned her head in the direction where she'd heard Lacy and Darius land. Sure enough, there they were, the two of them embracing in the darkness, smiling in relief that they were back together. "Damn, I feel fat in this place! It really is hell!"

Everett laughed, and Tracy smiled when she heard her sister laugh too as she approached them. Soon all four of them were laughing, even though Tracy could sense the apprehension in the air. They were all together, yeah. But where?! Would they ever get out of here?!

"Lacy," she said, slowly pulling away from Everett and turning to her sister. "Are you all right?"

"I . . . I think so," said Lacy, frowning as if she was trying to figure out the answer to Tracy's question. "What our parents said . . . it really got to me. But I feel all right now." She cocked her head and looked at Darius. Then she glanced back at Tracy and nodded. "I *am* all right. Sorry I pulled all you guys down here!"

"Way to go, sis," said Tracy, looking around in the heavy darkness. "Pulling us into the basement of hell. Nice job."

They all chuckled again, but the big question lingered over them like a dark cloud. They were here. They were together. But they were trapped. They were most certainly *not* all right! But if they'd been pulled to this sub-basement of the Darkness by accessing their own dark feelings of shame and guilt and everything in between, why didn't it feel horrible? Why did it feel like they were safe from the horror that surrounded them?!

And it was horror, Tracy realized as she squinted into the darkness and gasped when she realized that what she'd thought was a wall was in fact moving! At first she wondered if it was the Black Dragon, Murad's mate. But slowly she made out hands and legs, heads and bodies, butts and boobs, everything entwined like it was all part of one massive body. Then came the sounds: grunts, groans, moans, wails. Howls of ecstasy, but ecstasy that was hollow, pure carnal pleasure without the magic of human love.

"It's humans having sex like beasts," Tracy whispered as she moved close to her mate, feeling the dark energy of this place reaching out to her like invisible fingers. "That's what it is! And it feels . . . it feels sick! Ohmygod, I can't look!"

For a moment Tracy swore she saw their parents' twisted faces somewhere in the sea of enmeshed bodies, and she screamed and burrowed into her mate, shaking her head as she tried to get that image away from her! Beside her she could feel Lacy hugging Darius, and she instantly understood that the four of them were safe only because they were with their fated mates.

Slowly Tracy opened her eyes, and then she gasped when she saw that Lacy and Darius were shining with light once again! Desperately she looked up at her own mate, hoping to see the same light enveloping her too. But there was nothing. It didn't make sense! Wasn't that one kiss enough to bond them? Everett was her fat-

ed mate! What more did the Light need to forge
their eternal bond and keep them safe from the
Darkness? Did they actually need to have . . .

"Sex," came a voice from Tracy's left, and she
whipped her head around toward the sound.

"Who the hell are you?" Tracy groaned, blinking as the image of a curvy woman with brown
hair and the beautiful eyes of a fox shone through
the darkness. "Another demon? Another cousin
or aunt who did something horrible to get herself trapped in this sick place?"

"She's a Fox Shifter!" whispered Everett after a
moment. "And her scent . . . I swear it's familiar,
even though I don't recognize her face."

"A Fox Shifter and a Dark Witch," came Lacy's
voice, her tone tinged with relief. "Magda! You
found us!"

"It wasn't easy, but yes," said the Fox Shifter
with a smile that seemed oddly hesitant, even
though her eyes were beaming. "Thankfully you
guys left a lot of blood for me to use as I experi-
mented to find the right spells!"

"Oh, wow," said Lacy, touching the side of her
head as if checking for a wound. "That's great!
Sorry if we freaked you guys out with that dou-
ble-suicide thing. But I had faith that your magic

was strong enough to bring us back." She looked up at Darius and smiled, and Tracy could feel the bond her sister had with her mate—a bond that she knew was stronger than what she had with Everett right then.

Once again the thought swirled through her mind that the kiss had connected them, but their bond wasn't complete, their union wasn't sealed, their mating still unfinished. She frowned at the thought, feeling a strange rush of anger go through her. Why *wasn't* a kiss enough? Did they really need to actually do the deed to complete their bond?! Couldn't they unite in pure love without sex?!

"The Shifter is a union of flesh and spirit, human and animal, pure love and pure lust," came Magda's reply as if the witch could see Tracy's thoughts, understand her anger. "We are driven by a need to balance these basic forces of the universe even as these urges threaten to rip us apart. It's a curse, and that's why Shifters are blessed with the promise of fated mates." Magda sighed, her fox's eyes narrowing as she glanced around them. "Of course, fate doesn't come without faith. We are surrounded by the souls of Shifters who lost faith in the promise of their true mate. Shifters who lost the internal battle for balance and gave in to their urges to mate outside the fated bond." She sighed again, turning those wily fox's eyes back towards Tracy . "And the key word is mate. The two of you are connected, but the bond has to be completed, sealed, consummated. Without that completed bond, my magic won't work to bring you back to the world of flesh and blood."

"Wait, what?" Lacy snapped, pulling away from Darius and stepping in front of Tracy. "What do you mean, Magda?" She looked down at herself and frowned, her mouth slowly opening in muted shock as her body began to shimmer and then slowly fade. "Magda, no! I'm not leaving here without Tracy! I came here for my sister, and I'm *not* leaving without her!"

"There's nothing more you two can do," whispered Magda, her fox's eyes glowing red as magic flowed through her like a river. "The two of you helped Tracy and Everett connect with their pasts, understand who they were as individuals. The rest of their journey has to be completed on their own, as a couple." She blinked her glowing eyes, glancing down at Lacy's belly, which Tracy suddenly noticed was popping out in a beautifully pregnant curve! "Now you two have to complete your own journey as a couple. And that has to be done in the world of flesh and blood!"

"No!" screamed Lacy, trying to clutch at her sister's arms even as her body faded. "Darius, stop her! We're not done here! We have to travel to the Light and find the she-Dragon's human soul! That still has to be done!"

"Yes, it does," whispered Magda. "But that is now a task for your sister and her mate. The bobcat and the tiger. Their journey as a couple is tied to the task set before them. You cannot complete the task for them. It is their fate, not yours."

"I'm not leaving my sister here alone," said Lacy firmly, gritting her teeth like she was clamping down with all her will, slowing down Magda's magic.

But then Everett stepped forward, shaking his head, his long black hair waving fiercely in the darkness, his skin looking so bronze that even as a human he was blazing orange and black like a tiger. "She isn't alone," he said with a quiet confidence that almost shattered Tracy. "She'll never be alone again." He glanced over at Darius, and then down at the curve of Lacy's belly. "The witch is right. The two of you need to return before it's too late. Before you lose your own bond."

Lacy frowned as she followed Everett's gaze down to her belly. Then she gasped, cradling herself and staring down as her belly seemed to get larger and larger! "What's happening, Magda? We've only been here a few hours! I can't already be . . ."

"A few hours?!" said Magda, shaking her head and chuckling. "Lacy, time doesn't work the same way outside the world of flesh and blood. It might have felt like a few hours to you, but it's been nine months on Earth, Lacy! If you don't return now, your children will be born in this place!" The Fox-Shifter blinked, a flash of fear in her red eyes. "And even I don't know what will happen then. All I know is that I can't let it happen."

Tracy felt the truth of Magda's words, felt the urgency of the situation. It should have driven her nuts, but for some reason she felt calm. She looked up at Everett, standing tall and strong beside her. He was her future, Tracy understood. The witch was right. She and Everett had to complete the rest of the journey alone, as a couple. Every fated couple's journey was unique, and this was theirs: To navigate through this place beyond death, find their way back to life, find their own way home.

"Go," she whispered to her sister. "Go now, sis. You've gotten me this far, and now it's my time." She looked up at Everett, nodding and then slipping her arm into his, feeling the blazing warmth of his tiger envelop her in the cold darkness that surrounded them. "It's *our* time."

And then she couldn't speak, because just as Lacy, Darius, and Magda faded away from sight, her own sight was blocked out by a flash of orange and black.

It was Everett, eyes shining with need, his body telling her that yes, it was time. It was *their* time.

Then he kissed her.

By God, he kissed her.

12

Everett felt the weight of his body crash into Tracy, his lips pressing against hers, his tongue pushing deep into her mouth as he let his need take over. At the back of his mind he knew that this was dangerous, that they were in that place within the Darkness where they could stay in human form. In the background he could hear those soulless Shifters moan and wail as if it was a recording, a twisted soundtrack to their mating.

"Everett," Tracy gasped as she broke from the kiss, her eyes rolling back in her head as he held her tight against his naked body. She felt heavy, beautifully full and heavy, and he just growled and kissed her again, pressing his cock against her soft mound until he felt her heat, her wetness, her need.

"That is my name," he grunted, licking her face, her neck, even her ears as he squeezed her ass from behind, pulling her big buttocks apart with his strong fingers. "Just like your name is Eliza."

She giggled, wriggled, and then moaned as Everett ran his fingers up along her rear crack, his cock pressed lengthwise between their bodies. He could feel her wetness ooze from her slit like a lazy river, coating his balls and dripping down to the invisible ground.

"I can't believe you tried to name me," she whispered, running her fingers through his thick hair. "That's arrogance, plain and simple." Tracy smiled, but her smile faded as those background sounds rose up around them like someone had jacked up the volume. "And so is this," she whispered, blinking as she turned her head while pulling closer to him. "What are we doing, Everett? Is this going to free us or doom us forever? This place . . . Everett, this place is . . ."

"This place is the *only* place," whispered Everett. "The only place we can stay human, stay in the physical, be in the flesh. You heard what the dark witch said: We have to complete our bond in the flesh. The Shifter is human and animal in one, and there's no escaping the needs of the flesh. We're trapped here anyway. This is our only chance to get out, to travel back to the Light, to complete our task."

Those twisted souls in the background howled and whistled, clapping their hands like some deranged audience of demons. Everett wasn't sure if it was real or just some manifestation of their own shame, the shame they'd reclaimed just to get down to this place.

He felt Tracy struggle in his arms, like she was losing her nerve, focusing on the sounds of chaos around them. A chill came over him as he felt her breaking away from him, like her doubt and shame was pulling her away, pulling her towards that dark place. He could feel her body go cold against his, and he kissed her again, pulling her in as he tried to reclaim her like this was a fight! But her lips felt cool against his, and Everett gritted his teeth as he realized that this wasn't going to be easy. The Darkness was fighting them like it was a living, breathing thing. He could feel the lust between him and his mate, smell the needs of their flesh. But it felt hollow without the warmth of human love, and Everett leaned his head back and roared in anguish. What was missing?! What more could they do?! How could he break free from the clutches of this Darkness? How could he expect to win in this hostile territory, where the forces of Darkness seemed overwhelming, were already overwhelming his mate?! Was he not strong enough? What was missing?! *What*?!

Surrender, came a whisper from somewhere far away, and Everett knew it was his tiger. *You have to surrender to the Darkness. Remember, Darkness is part of the Shifter's essence. It is the essence of the animal, and it has to be faced and brought into balance by the human. Your problem is you are reaching for human love in a place where it cannot exist. You are trying to reject the Darkness in you, which is an impossible task, an unwinnable fight. You must surrender to the Darkness, and trust that you both will find your way back to the Light, find your way to balance, to harmony, to peace. Peace only comes after the battle is won. And the tiger does not win a battle by barreling straight ahead like a dumb bear or screaming in like a fire-breathing dragon. The ti-*

ger hunts at night. It uses the Darkness as an ally. Use the Darkness, Everett. Use the Darkness to set yourself free, to set us all free. Use the Darkness.

Everett looked around wildly, images of those twisted human souls coming through the Darkness, a wall of bodies, glistening black, arms and legs entwined, groping, grasping, rubbing, clutching, with moans of hollow ecstasy and wails of feral need punctuating the surreal scene. Surrender? Surrender to *this*? No!

"Everett, no," came Tracy's whisper, and Everett frowned as he felt his mate try to pull away from him. Immediately he knew his tiger was right, that they couldn't find human love in a place where that power didn't exist, *couldn't* exist. They were fighting the very nature of the universe, fighting their own nature, trying to reject the essence of what they were: Light *and* Darkness.

"Everett, no," she groaned again as Everett dug his fingers into the soft flesh of her rump, feeling himself slowly open up to the truth of his own being, the Darkness of his own essence. "Everett, look. Look!"

Everett glanced up at where Tracy was pointing, his eyes going wide as he saw a tunnel of light slowly open up through the Darkness. What the hell? Was this a way out? A way back to that place of Light they'd glimpsed earlier, where Tracy saw her beloved mountains and he saw the sweeping grasslands of the majestic savannah? But was that really a true vision, Everett wondered as he thought back to how he'd seen those two Bear Shifters emerge from the dark cluster of trees in that place.

Tracy was reaching for that tunnel of Light, but Everett was holding on to her, his mind racing as he tried to decide what to do. Somehow he knew that his next choice was critical, and as he stared up at the Light, he remembered how he and Tracy had felt their need rise when they were in what they thought was heaven, how they'd found themselves back in that pit, back in animal form, amongst the Shifter animals who'd died unmated.

"Tracy, it's an illusion," he whispered. "We can't go back there without completing our bond. And this is the only place where we can complete our bond in the flesh. We have to stay here. There's no shortcut to the Light, Tracy. We have to take the long road. Through the Darkness. It's part of us, and we can't escape it. We'll just find ourselves back in that pit again and again until we face who we are, what we are, *why* we are!"

"You're crazy," Tracy screamed, reaching towards that tunnel of Light with one arm, clawing at his face and neck with the other. "I see my mountains, Everett! We can go there, live there forever!"

"Forever unbalanced," said Everett, his determination rising as Tracy slashed at his face with her nails. "Tracy, if we go to the Light without completing our bond, it will split our animals away from us forever. We'll truly be dead. We'll be dead like any other Shifter that died unmated. We'll have failed at our task. We have to do this here. We have to do this now."

Do it, snarled his Tiger from what seemed like a million miles away.*Take her before you lose her. If she goes to the Light, her animal and her human will be split forever. It has already been too long for you both. The forces of the universe are splitting us all apart, and now it's up to you. Take her like a tiger takes its prey in the night. Give in to the Darkness, or else she will be forever lost to the Light, just like Sinesta.*

"Who the hell is Sinesta?" growled Everett, blinking as he struggled to hold his mate back. "And how the hell can someone be *lost* to the Light! The Light is . . . is *heaven*, isn't it?"

Sinesta is Murad's mate, whispered his tiger. *And*

to find her you have to let go of the human ideas of heaven and hell, good and evil, darkness and light. The words you use make you believe that Light is desirable and Darkness is to be avoided. But remember your essence, your true nature, the true nature of the universe and everything in it. Our mate is scared of the Darkness. She thinks it is an evil force that is somewhere out there. She is a strong-willed woman, and even though her animal is trying to tell her what I am telling you, it isn't getting through. Her animal is a bobcat—powerful but also skittish by nature. Her human is winning the battle, but she doesn't realize that what she thinks is winning is actually losing. If her human finds its way to the Light, it will leave its animal behind. So take her, Everett. Take her like a tiger takes its mate, like a tiger seizes its fate. The hunt is over. Remind her what she is.

"Remind her what she is . . ." Everett repeated absentmindedly as he felt her nails draw blood on his face and neck. He licked his lips and growled, the taste of blood reminding him what *he* was: A hunter. A killer. A beast. A creature of the night. A being of both Light and Darkness.

"Remember what you are," he growled as he tightened his grip around her waist until she finally went limp in his arms, unable to fight him any longer. He reached around the back of her neck, digging his fingers into her hair, closing his fist around the roots of her thick tresses, forcing her to look into his eyes. "You're a woman and an animal. You're Light and Darkness. And you're my mate, Tracy. You're my mate, and I'm going to take you."

He kissed her hard on the mouth, the blood on his lips mixing with her saliva as her eyes flicked wide open and then slowly fluttered closed. She was trying to say something, but Everett didn't give a damn. He understood that this wasn't the time for conversation, that words and speech were the enemy in this place where the flesh reigned supreme. He had to take her quick, take her hard, take her like a tiger takes its prey.

Without hesitation he reached between their bodies, his other hand holding her tight by the hair. He could feel the outer lips of her vagina throb against the back of his hand, and he fiercely rubbed her mound and fingered her until she opened up for him.

Then he grasped his cock and lined its massive head against her slit, kissed her one more time, and then drove himself into her, all the way deep, all the damned way.

13

I'm being taken, she thought as she felt Everett drive up into her, his cock pushing so deep she almost choked. Taken by the tiger.

And it was the tiger taking her, she understood, screaming as she felt his power, gasping in shock as sensations of such pure ecstasy rolled through her that she thought she might die. Her flesh felt alive with energy, and she could hear her bobcat wailing in the distance. The feeling of her animal startled her, and it was only then that Tracy realized that it had been missing all this while, like it had been lost, separated, split apart.

You dumb bitch, roared her cat, its voice thick with fury, wild with indignation. *You were gonna leave me to rot alone in the Darkness while you selfishly reached for the Light! Thank God for our Tiger! Now close your eyes and open your legs! We don't have much time! You need to be taken now, taken hard, and taken fast.*

Tracy blinked in confusion as she felt her bobcat retreat after it had vented, and suddenly she felt a wave of relief wash through her. She glanced up at that tunnel of Light, smiling as she realized that the human in her had been reaching for it but the animal couldn't follow unless her fated bond was complete. If she'd managed to get to the Light, it would have split her cat from her forever! Her Tiger saved her!

"My tiger," she groaned, digging her nails into Everett's strong back as he lifted her off her feet and began to bounce her on his cock so hard she could barely breathe. The pace was furious, relentless, manic with urgency, and Tracy could feel the fever rise in her body as she opened up to him, to her animal's needs, to the Darkness.

Suddenly she was coming, reaching climax so fast she screamed in shock! Her orgasm rolled through her like a freight train, and then Everett was coming too, letting out a guttural roar as he exploded deep inside her, blasting his seed so far inside her she swore she could taste it in her throat.

At first she didn't understand, but as Everett pumped the rest of his hot semen into her, making her pussy clench as she milked him dry like a wanton woman of the night, she understood the urgency, understood why their first coupling had happened so fast, with such quickness. It was the tiger's way. It was how a tiger hunted. No hesitation at the moment of truth. No chance for escape.

She wailed as she came again, feeling Everett's seed blast into her like a geyser erupting into the sky. She closed her eyes and howled, and in her mind she thought she could see her womb taking his seed, seven strong swimmers breaking through her barrier, fertilizing her like the rain gives life to the ready soil. Her mind spun as a vision of seven kittens came to her clear as day, and she cried as she realized she was looking upon her own unborn children, a litter of kittens that were not here yet but had somehow *always* been there!

Suddenly she was blinded by a flash of the brightest light, and she screamed as she felt herself being pulled at the speed of thought. She shouted for Everett, terrified that she was being split from him, but when she managed to open her eyes she saw that telltale golden thread connecting her to him, joining them together, now and for eternity.

"Look! No hands!" she squealed, feeling the rush of her climax transform into a spiritual joy with effortless ease as the two of them spun through the universe, connected by that unbreakable bond. She could see their animals spinning along with them, the bobcat and the tiger mewling and growling, purring in delight, pawing at each other in play.

They spun through starlight and moonlight, past the sun and the solar system like it was all part of a magical ride. She could see every event of time and space like moving billboards as she merrily rode along with her mate. She could see her sister back safely in the "real" world, Lacy cursing and clawing at her mate Darius as she gave birth to her own babies! She could see the other Shifters of her newfound crew watching anxiously, Magda the Witch with tears in her eyes as her shoulders slumped in relief at being able to bring Lacy and Darius back in time.

Somewhere else she could see Murad's Black Dragon flying silently through night-skies, ominous and dark like a demon on the hunt. But Tracy was still smiling even though she knew there was still a task for her and Everett to complete.

"There's more to our destiny than just each other," she whispered, both for herself and for Everett. She smiled again as she watched the group of Shifters on that moving billboard of her dream. Each of them had been chosen. They were all special. And each of them had to accept the greater responsibility that came with having the power of both human and animal, Light and Dark.

She whipped her head to the left, distracted by a screech that she knew was Murad's mate, the Black she-Dragon who'd swallowed them whole, sent them on this journey, was waiting for them to get back. She could feel its impatience, its restlessness, its dark fury slowly building as it manifested itself on Earth. She understood the urgency, but it didn't make her anxious. She was bonded with her mate. She'd found her fate. One battle was won, and although the war was still raging, the final battle would have to wait.

"Because this is *our* time," she whispered to her mate, reaching out her hand as Everett grinned and flew over to her like he had the wings of an angel. "It's *our* time."

14

This is *our* time, Everett thought as he watched his mate raise her arms and spin through the air like a snowflake, her body bathed in golden light. He could see the strand of pure energy connecting the two of them, a golden rope tethering them together. In the distance he could still hear the howls of those humans trapped in the Darkness. He could still hear the growls of the animals doomed to that other part of the Darkness. But he could also feel the melancholy of the humans who existed in the Light, the souls of Shifters who'd died without finding their mates.

"You see that, Tracy?" he whispered to his mate, pointing in the direction of that melancholic sensation like it was a real place. "You feel that?"

Tracy turned in the air like a feather, and they both looked into the distance, staring at what looked like a dense point of light no bigger than a dot. But as they stared the dot grew larger, until they were gazing upon an island, an island shining with light. On the island roamed the human souls of Shifters who'd died without finding their mates, and Tracy clutched Everett's arm as the two of them drew close enough to feel the strange desolation that racked these souls.

"I know the vision isn't real," Tracy whispered as they watched the humans mill about with plastic smiles on their faces. They were all naked, but their bodies were smooth and hairless, with no visible sex organs. They were all shimmering with light but still missing something. Missing something essential. Lacking a warmth that Tracy could feel burning strong in her own body. A warmth that she suddenly understood came from the Darkness, from the flesh not the spirit, from the purity of lust not the magic of love. "Oh, Everett," she whispered. "All this while I thought the Light was a place of infinite happiness, boundless joy. But in a way it's no different from the Darkness, is it? In a way it's even *darker* than the Darkness! Is this really heaven?! What about the myths we all grew up with? The age-old stories that every civilization passes down about the wonderful afterlife? Is it all a lie?!"

Everett shook his head, taking her hand firmly in his, sending a shiver through Tracy as she felt their union of spirit and body so clearly it almost made her cry.

"Not for humans, it isn't," he said firmly, his fiery eyes narrowing as he glanced past the shimmering island towards another rapidly expanding dot of light. "For humans the afterlife *is* what the myths and legends and prophets promised through the ages. Look over there, Tracy. Those are human souls. Pure human."

Tracy gasped when she looked over at the scene emerging from that second dot of light. Everett was right! This looked like the heaven she'd imagined might exist, the heaven described in old myths and paintings, by folks who'd had near-death experiences, by every soothsayer and prophet throughout time. These human souls were laughing and smiling, some of them wearing the finest clothes, other strolling naked without shame like it was all a joke, some enjoying fruit and berries, others eating popcorn and candy, some smoking cigarettes, others doing pushups and jumping jacks. It seemed like everyone was doing whatever the hell they wanted, but the energy emanating wasn't evil. From where she stood it seemed pure and clean. No guilt. No shame. No regrets.

Tracy instinctively scanned all around her, cocking her head as she turned back to Everett. "But if this is heaven for human souls, then where is their hell? These souls seem to be enjoying things that they shouldn't be enjoying, things that should make them impure! So if this is heaven for them, what is hell?"

"Isn't it obvious?" said Everett with a slow smile. "Earth itself is hell! Earth is where a human forgets he has an immortal soul, is forced to confront the limitations of his body, is constantly being told that he is shameful, sinful, useless. And then when he gets past that struggle, he ascends to heaven, where he is free from guilt, free from shame, free from negativity." His smile faded as he turned back to the island of Light, the place where the listless human souls of Shifters were milling about aimlessly like zombie-angels. "But for a Shifter, *Earth* is heaven! Earth is the only place where a Shifter can be in balance, where animal and human can be joined, be in eternal balance, enjoy the equally pure pleasures of the mind and the body, the spirit and the flesh."

"But . . . but humans are animals too, aren't they? They have to struggle to find that same balance between dark and light, don't they?"

Everett nodded. "But the conflict isn't as strong in a pureblood human. The conflict between its animal nature and the intellectual needs of the mind isn't as strong. Evolution took care of that."

"Evolution? Like how?" said Tracy, turning towards her mate as she remembered that this man had spent years studying, that he was a beast with a brain. But so was she, and she squinted as she tried to get her head around what Everett was saying.

"Think about it," Everett said, putting his arm around her, his face beaming as if he was pleasantly surprised that she was curious enough to ask him to explain. It almost bugged her, and she frowned as she wondered if he'd thought she was some dumb bimbo all this while. Then she lost the frown and chastised herself for using the word bimbo. Just because a woman had boobs didn't mean she was dumb. Besides, she was too fat to be a bimbo. 36-23-36 were classic bimbo stats. She was more like 38-32-43 or something awful like that.

Tracy blinked as she felt self-consciousness ripple through her. Was that even possible? She was bonded with her true mate, wasn't she? And he was clearly attracted to her—shit, she could still feel his seed inside her, he'd poured so much up there! She blinked again, trying to ignore the strange mix of indignation and self-consciousness that was messing with her peace. Finally she forced herself to smile and listen to Everett's explanation.

"Evolution has lifted humans past the needs of just the animal," Everett said, his voice sounding annoyingly pedantic, like he was lecturing her as if she was dumb as a rock. "Think about it: Humans these days can be perfectly fulfilled and happy without ever having children. Sure, most humans do feel the need to reproduce, but the human mind has developed to the point where that

sexual energy can be diverted into other meaningful pursuits. Don't you know men and wom-
en who've chosen not to start families, dedicat-
ing their lives to some higher, broader purpose?"

Tracy frowned as she touched her belly, that image she'd seen earlier of her seven kittens coming
back with a vividness that made her breath catch.
She looked up at her mate, frowning when she
saw how excited he'd gotten talking about some
"higher" purpose of the human spirit!

"So you believe that wanting to have kids is
a *lower* purpose? If a woman chooses to dedicate
her life to raising children it means she's some
unambitious loser?" She snorted, pushing his arm
off her as that perversely confusing indignation
rose up in her again. "I thought you were a tiger,
but you're just another pig. Shoulda known."

"*Shoulda*?" said Everett, his eyes narrowing, his
face darkening, his mouth twisting into a sneer.
He folded his muscular arms across his bare chest
and looked down his nose at her. "Is that a word
in the English language, Eliza?!"

"Call me that again," Tracy snarled, feeling her
bobcat come alive within her, the animal burning
with what she could tell was the same perverse
energy that was making her snap at her mate

even though she knew she was purposely misinterpreting what he was saying. It was almost like she was itching for a fight. What was happening to her?! To them both?! "Go on," she hissed, backing away from him and baring her teeth. "Call me Eliza again! I dare you!"

Everett had turned to face her dead on, his eyes blazing fierce orange, his tiger burning bright within him in a way that scared Tracy. "Say *shoulda* one more time," he growled, baring his own teeth. "Go on, Eliza. I dare you."

"Coulda, woulda, *shoulda*!" screamed Tracy, feeling her anger mount like she couldn't stop it. It scared her as much as it confused her. Were they *fighting*?! About what? Was she crazy?! They'd just completed their fated bond! She was pregnant with his tiger cubs! They were bonded forever in a cosmic marriage, tethered by an unbreakable rope of golden light!

Then from the corner of her eye she sensed movement. She turned, her eyes narrowed as she faced that island of lost Shifter human souls. Those souls were milling about just like before, except for one that was standing fixed on the edge of the island, looking up as if gazing at the stars. As if by magic, Tracy felt her vision zoom in on the soul until she could tell it was a woman. A woman with dark red hair like flames that had died out. A woman with dark eyes that looked misted over and sightless, like she'd been blinded by cataracts.

Tracy frowned as a chill rose up along her spine. In the background she could tell that Everett had seen the woman too, so this wasn't some personal vision of Tracy's.

"What's she looking at?" Tracy whispered, feeling her dread rise as a crooked smile began to break on the blind woman's face.

Everett was silent for a moment. Then he reached for her hand and gripped it tight, his voice coming as a low whisper. "Us, Tracy. She's looking at us."

And just as he said it, the woman's eyes flicked wide open, those cataracts disappearing to reveal green eyes that shone like emeralds on fire. She raised her right arm, that crooked smile widening as she pointed at Tracy and Everett like she could see them!

"Sinesta," Everett muttered, pulling Tracy closer to his body as if to shield her.

"Who the hell is Sinesta?" Tracy said even though she knew the answer. This was the Black she-Dragon's human side. "Oh, shit! We found her, Everett! We found her!"

But Everett was tense as a slab of stone by her side, his eyes fixed on the green-eyed woman who was still pointing at them. It was only when Tracy felt a strange pull that she realized Sinesta wasn't pointing. Sinesta was reaching out. Reaching for that golden thread that connected Tracy and Everett. The golden thread that was now a bridge between Light and Darkness. An open road for someone who knew how to travel it.

"We didn't find her," Everett muttered, shaking his head and smiling grimly. "*She* found *us*!"

Tracy felt herself choke as she watched Sinesta firmly grasp that golden rope and hoist herself up like she was a gymnast, swinging herself off the island, her sinister smile widening as she narrowed her green eyes at Tracy and cocked her head at a sickeningly unnatural angle.

"What . . . what is she, Everett?" Tracy whispered as Sinesta hung on that rope of light like some kind of mythical bird. As she watched, Sinesta began to change form, her hair turning bright red, her breasts emerging from her flat, asexual chest—heavy breasts with big nipples that were dark red and oozing with what looked like milk! The sight terrified Tracy, but she couldn't turn her eyes away, staring in shock as Sinesta's sex emerged like it had been cut into her by an invisible sculptor. "Ohmygod, Everett! Is she . . . is she giving birth?!"

Sinesta opened her mouth and screamed like she herself was just being born, and Tracy screamed too when she saw Sinesta spread her legs wide and push out a child . . . a child with one green eye and one gold eye, a child with the wings of a dragon, gold and green wings that were torn and broken, hanging limp from the child's back.

"It's Adam Drake," whispered Everett slowly. "She's reliving the birth of her son, Tracy! That must be when Murad tried to Turn her! She must have been killed while giving birth, and she's been trapped in that moment of pain and joy, reliving it again and again until it twisted her into this . . . this creature!"

"So what is she?" Tracy asked again, watching agape as the child withered away into nothing and disappeared, leaving nothing but Sinesta's mournful howl.

"I don't know," said Everett, and Tracy could

hear the tiger in his voice. "But whatever she is, she needs to be put down. Put down before she finds her way to the Darkness. Finds her way back to her dragon." He shook his head, slowly letting go of her hand as if he was preparing to Change to his tiger. "We thought reuniting Sinesta with her dragon would bring balance to the Black she-dragon, eventually bring balance to a lopsided world. But Sinesta is too far gone. What happened to her corrupted the human in her. She isn't human anymore. Reuniting her with her dragon can't balance the beast. It will only create a new kind of beast!"

Tracy felt herself torn as she watched Sinesta scream again, her breastmilk turning blood-red as she pushed out another child from her womb, another Adam Drake, broken and bruised, torn and twisted, dead before the cord was cut.

"It doesn't make sense," Tracy muttered, narrowing her eyes as she tried to understand what the green-eyed Sinesta was going through. "Adam Drake is alive and well. He didn't die in childbirth. So why is Sinesta reliving something that never happened?"

Then as if the universe had heard Tracy's question, the answer came flashing through in a vision so vivid that even Everett shouted in surprise. She watched as the vision grew so bright it was all they could see, and then in flash it was gone again.

But that snapshot into Sinesta's past had been enough, and Tracy screamed as she understood. Then the tears came, and Tracy wept for Sinesta even as she smiled with the faith that everything was going to be all right. There was hope for Sinesta. She'd just been twisted by what had happened to her during childbirth!

"She didn't know Murad was a dragon at all!" Everett gasped, looking at Tracy and then back at Sinesta. "So when Adam was born, she thought she'd given birth to some kind of monster! And she . . . oh, God, Tracy, she . . ."

"She tried to kill her own son," whispered Tracy as she slowly processed the enormity of their shared vision. "Murad intervened! Or rather, his dragon burst forth and killed its mate to protect its offspring! Which means Murad's Black Dragon isn't roaming the earth because it's all lovesick and moody as it searches for its long-lost true love! It hates its true mate for trying to kill his son! And Sinesta hates him back! There's no chance for reconciliation! There's no chance for balance! If Sinesta and her dragon manifest on Earth, the two Black Dragons will be at each other's throats!"

The realization made her sick to the stomach, and Tracy felt despair cut through her like a jagged-edged knife. At first she'd thought she could just tell Sinesta that her son was alive and well, but Sinesta knew that already. She didn't *want* her son alive and well! She believed he was a monster! She believed her mate was a demon!

"But what about yourself?" Tracy whispered without thinking, looking deep into Sinesta's eyes. "What do you believe about yourself, Sinesta? You're a mother. Does it matter if you gave birth to a monster? He's yours, and it's your fate to love your child no matter what. It's your fate and your duty. There's no escaping it, Sinesta! Accept your son into your heart. Accept that he came from your womb, that he's a part of you. Accept him and love him!"

Sinesta's head cocked the other way, her green eyes flickering as she looked at Tracy like Tracy was speaking some strange language. Again Tracy saw movement on their left, and when she turned she was astonished to see that vision of

human heaven that she and Everett had marveled at earlier!

"Sinesta?" Tracy said, her eyes widening when
she saw one of those human souls—a woman in
a long, flowing dress, red hair healthy and strong,
green eyes clear and focused. "Ohmygod, how can
you be here and there?"

"Bloody hell," Everett whispered. "Her human
soul must have been split just like her dragon and
human got split! A three-way split! After all, Sinesta wasn't a Shifter! When a human dies, they go
to that happy place in the Light where all human
souls go. But Murad's attack also Turned Sinesta
in the moment of death, so not only did it create that Black she-Dragon, it also created some
kind of semi-human soul that was trapped in
the place of Light where unmated Shifters send
their humans! "

Tracy looked back and forth between the two
Sinestas, understanding in a flash what Everett
meant. "So I'm trying to reason with the wrong
Sinesta?" she said, glancing at the human Sinesta and then towards the semi-human splinter of
a soul that was hanging like a deranged monkey
from that golden thread. "Wait, where'd she go?!"

"Bloody hell!" Everett roared, twisting his head around as he tried to find the dark Sinesta.

"Everett, look!" Tracy shouted, pointing towards where the human Sinesta had been looking up at them. Except now the human soul of Sinesta was walking away. She'd turned her back on them like she didn't want anything to do with this drama. It was like she'd found her way to heaven, and so to hell with everyone else! "Sinesta, no! You can't turn your back on this! You're turning your back on yourself! You'll never find peace if you don't help us!"

"I've found my peace," came Sinesta's voice even as her soul twirled around in the light like it was dancing. "I married a monster. I gave birth to a monster. And I was killed by a monster. I've paid my dues, and this is my reward."

"Tracy," Everett shouted, grabbing her hand and pulling. "Forget her! We need to go to the Darkness and stop that other Sinesta before she merges with her dragon!"

"Good luck killing something that's already dead," said Sinesta, still twirling around in her peaceful little heaven. "Now shoo, you monsters. I've got to dance my way through eternity. Shoo, I say!"

"*You're* the monster!" Tracy shrieked, feeling her anger rise as she suddenly understood that even this so-called "human" heaven was colored by her own childish notions about heaven being some place of boundless joy. Both she and Everett had been wrong. They'd all been wrong—even Sinesta! "You think just because you don't have wings or claws or fangs or fur you're not a monster? Hah! Look at yourself, woman! You didn't know that Murad was a dragon?! *Bullshit*! You knew! You knew and you chose to deny it." Tracy breathed deep as the words flowed like she was seeing it all clearly in her mind. "And that was the*right* choice, Sinesta! Murad was your fated mate, and you chose to look past the monster in him, to accept your fate! But you were still just a human, still plagued with the guilt and shame of being attracted to a creature that anyone else would call a demon. The conflict broke you, Sinesta. You were a splintered soul before Murad killed you. Help us, Sinesta. Help us put you back together again."

Everett had stopped trying to pull her away, and when Tracy glanced at him she blinked when she saw how he was looking at her. There was real admiration in his eyes, like he was moved by what she'd said. She smiled at him, blinking again and then turning back to Sinesta.

"How can I be put together again when I was never even whole?" Sinesta whispered.

"None of us was whole until we found each other," said Everett, his voice steady and quiet, his body warm and protective as he stood close to Tracy and slid his arm around her waist. "All of us have many sides. Each of us is a complex being of both Light and Darkness. Finding our true mates is just one part of our journey."

"So what's the other part?" said Sinesta, her voice trembling as if she was allowing herself to open up in ways that had been closed for years, perhaps forever.

"Finding our place in the world," whispered Everett. "Accepting our responsibility to not just our mates and family, but to our community, to the world, to the universe itself. That's the responsibility of the Shifter, Sinesta."

"But I'm not . . ." Sinesta began to say, frowning as if their words were getting through.

"Yes, you are," said Tracy. "You *are* a Shifter, Sinesta. You *did* get Turned. So whether you like it or not, that Black she-Dragon is your responsibility. It's *you*."

"I didn't ask for that!" Sinesta shot back. "I didn't ask for any of this!"

"Neither did we," said Everett. "But that doesn't change a thing. It's still our responsibility. After all, that's what fate means."

Tracy glanced over at her mate, half-smiling as she wondered if she should poke him for saying that he didn't ask to be bonded with her. But she knew what he meant. She understood what he meant. But did Sinesta understand? Would she accept her responsibility to tame her own dragon? Why would she? She was in heaven, wasn't she? Dancing merrily through the clouds or whatever?

But even as the thought crossed Tracy's mind, a dark shadow seemed to pass over that place where Sinesta stood. At first Tracy thought it was the Black she-Dragon flying out of the Darkness, re-united with that twisted version of Sinesta. But then she realized that it was a shadow that was passing over that so-called heaven where Sinesta had been dancing like a dervish.

"That's not heaven," Tracy blurted out. She scanned the other human spirits in that place, and she shook her head as the realization dawned on her. Yes, the souls there were happy, but they were not free. They were still trapped by their attachments to the world of flesh and blood! Why else were they amusing themselves by wearing fine clothes, eating and smoking, drinking and dancing? "It's just a way-station, some in-between place where souls are learning about the afterlife. That's why so many are fixated on what brought them physical joy on Earth. To move on, they need to let go of those attachments." She focused back on Sinesta, who had turned away from them again and had struck up her dance once more.

"It's no use, Tracy," said Everett, sighing as they watched Sinesta twist and twirl her way through the party in the clouds. "Her only attachment seems to be to what must have brought her joy on Earth."

"Dancing?" said Tracy with a frown. "So we're just gonna let her dance away into the fluffy clouds while her dark Dragon burns the world to a crisp?"

"Nope," said Everett with a grin. He glanced at the golden rope tethering the two of them and shrugged. "We're going to complete our task. We're going to bring her back to her dragon."

Tracy stared up at Everett. "Um, are you saying we're going to kidnap a human soul from the afterlife and feed it to a dark, feral dragon?"

Everett shrugged. "That's exactly what I'm saying, dear Eliza. You in?"

Tracy shook her head in disbelief. Then a smile broke and she shrugged too. "Yeah, I'm in. After all, that's what fate means, right?"

15

After all, that's what fate means, right?

Everett grinned as he took his mate's hand and dove down to that place where Sinesta was dancing the day away. He knew that they probably didn't need to "fly" down there like superheroes, but it seemed appropriate under the circumstances.

"Whee!" said Tracy from beside them as they blasted through a cloud barrier that smelled like lavender, the two of them hand in hand, buck naked and shameless. "Hello, people! Don't worry! We're just passing through!"

But the human souls seemed oblivious to the two flying cat-Shifters, and as Everett grasped Tracy's hand and brought her down for a smooth landing, he realized that the souls were oblivious of one another too! What had looked like some big party was in fact a group of disconnected souls, unable to see each other!

A strange sense of desolation washed over Everett, and when he looked at his mate, he knew Tracy felt it too. Something had changed.

"What's changed?" Tracy asked as they stood on what felt like soft ground. "This place felt joyful when we were looking down from above. But now that we're here, it feels . . ."

"It feels dark," growled Everett, tightening his jaw as he felt his tiger stir inside him. "We need to hurry, Tracy. The Black Dragon is getting more out of balance. It must have consumed that twisted version of Sinesta."

He glanced down at the golden rope connecting the two of them together and stretching out to infinity beyond. It was still thick and strong, but it appeared to be tightening, like someone— or some*thing*—was pulling on it!

"Feels like it," Tracy said, noticing that the golden rope had gone taut. She reached for the rope and tugged on it three times. "Hold your horses! We're bringing her to you!"

Sinesta was still dancing in the distance, her eyes closed, mouth frozen in a smile, arms above her head as she twirled and twisted. Everett tried to grab her, but the golden rope was too tight, pulling him back like he was on a leash!

"Bloody hell," he muttered, looking back and frowning. "The Black she-Dragon is getting darker, more out of balance as it consumes all that hatred that the dark Sinesta carries with her. It's so far out of balance that maybe it doesn't *want* this part of its soul back! Tracy, give me your hand. This is gonna take our combined strength."

"*Gonna*?" said Tracy with a wry grin. She closed one eye and raised the other eyebrow. "Is that a word in the English language? How very improper of you!"

Everett felt a smile break as he locked his fingers with his mate's, feeling their connection counter the pull of the dark dragon. He took a breath and nodded at her, and they both stepped forward together as one, their combined power allowing them to move. Step by step they got closer even as the dragon tried to pull them back, pull them down to its dark place.

"One more step," Everett grunted, feeling every muscle in his body flexed to the max, his tiger roaring inside him, his mate with him every step of the way. "And gotcha!"

Both Everett and Tracy reached out their free hands at the same time, clamping down on Sinesta's arms and gripping tight. Time seemed to stand still in that moment, and the two Shifters glanced at each other.

"Um, now what?" said Tracy, blinking as she forced a smile.

"Now we fulfill our destiny," said Everett, gripping his mate's hand tight as he felt the dragon pull on their cosmic leash. "We put the pieces of Sinesta back together, bring the Black Dragon into balance, bring the entire world into balance. Then we go back to the world, have babies, and live happily ever after. After all, that's what fate means, right?"

"That sounds nice," said Tracy, taking a breath

and steadying herself as that rope got tighter, the tension building up to breaking point. "But are you sure there won't be another twist before we get to the happily ever after?"

Everett shrugged, and just then the dragon yanked all three of them back towards the Darkness, pulling them through space and time, through heaven and hell and everything in between. The two Shifters roared as they spun through space, both of them holding Sinesta's soul tight, all of them spinning . . . spinning . . . spinning . . . until they were covered in shadow, a shadow that felt like night itself.

It was the Black she-Dragon, and they were inside her belly once again, pulled back to where it all began for them! Everett looked over toward his mate to make sure she was all right, and he grinned when he saw her breathless and smiling, her face flushed with the excitement of their journey. Perhaps it was all in their heads, but bloody hell it felt good! It felt like this was right! Like they'd accomplished what they were chosen to do! Their task was complete, and now they would get their reward, find their peace, their happily-ever-after!

"Let go!" Everett roared to Tracy, nodding toward Sinesta, who looked oddly calm, like she'd gone into a trance or was perhaps passed out. "Give her back to the Black Dragon. We're done here, Tracy!"

Tracy nodded, releasing Sinesta just as Everett let go as well. The two Shifters were still holding each other's hands tight, and Everett glanced down at that shimmering golden rope that seemed to be shining so bright he wondered if it would burst into heavenly flames!

"Done? Really? Did we really just save the world?" Tracy squealed as the two of them kept spinning, this time up along the dragon's belly like it was getting ready to spit them out like a cat pops out a hairball! "No more twists? Happily ever after?"

"No more twists," said Everett with a calm confidence. He could feel his tiger's sense of control return in the most exhilarating way, and he knew it was content. The tiger had a preternatural sense of impending danger, and if it was calm, it meant the danger had passed. It wanted nothing more than to revel in the simple joy of being with its mate. Just the two of them. Always and forever.

And then the dragon coughed them out into the

open universe, and Everett closed his eyes and held his mate tight as they twisted and turned toward their happily ever after.

16

This is happiness, Tracy thought as she felt Everett's big hand hold hers as they spun through the ether, coughed out of a Black she-Dragon's mouth, complete and unbroken, their bond stronger than ever. We went to hell and back together, and we're still together. We'll always be together.

She looked over at Everett, smiling as she saw

his beautiful black hair flow like strands of pure energy, his eyes burning bright with his tiger's spirit, his naked body glowing with the golden light that surrounded the two of them. He was looking back at her, his eyes both focused on her and lost in her at the same time.

"What?" she said, blinking and looking away for a moment as they spun like golden snowflakes. "What are you looking at?"

"You," he said without hesitation. "Just you. It's been chaos from the moment we met, and I just want a moment to look at you, Tracy. To really look at you."

"Weirdo," she said with a self-conscious giggle that sent a shiver through her body, making her bobcat purr in the background. She could tell that her cat was bursting with joy, mewling as it basked in the pleasure of being so connected to its fated mate. She giggled again as Everett just stared at her, but she knew what he meant. They'd never really had a chance to just be a couple, had they? Everything about their courtship had been a whirlwind of urgency! They'd been killed after their first kiss! Even their first mating was filled with urgency! Then learning about their own pasts, facing the choices that their parents had made, finally facing Sinesta's splintered soul.

Now it's time to face him, my mate, my always and forever, Tracy thought as she looked back into Everett's eyes and smiled. She didn't feel the need to say a word. It didn't seem necessary. She already knew so much about his past, the kind of man he was, the kind of animal he was. Everything they'd gone through together had showed them each other's souls.

Exactly, whispered her cat from inside her. *Now show him your body, girl. Without shame. Without self-consciousness. Without thought. We are bonded mates, and we can travel freely through Light and Darkness. So experience that freedom. Enjoy that freedom. Discover what it truly means to be balanced, to be human and animal at once, to love both sides of yourself, both sides of ourselves.*

Tracy could feel her heat rising as her bobcat's whispers faded away. Everett's gaze was moving down along her curves, and she could feel his hunger rising, the need of the animal in him coming to the fore, taking over. Around her the universe was darkening, but it felt beautiful, safe, natural, and Tracy understood what her cat had meant. She had nothing to fear from the Darkness. She *was* the Darkness just like she was the Light, just like she was body and spirit, human and animal.

"Take me," she whispered, seeing the flame ignite in her mate's eyes as he reached across and grabbed her by the back of the neck, drawing her into his body. "Take me, Everett."

He kissed her just as she said it, the energy of the kiss making her world explode from the inside, sending her spinning away as their lips locked, their tongues touched, their bodies merged like they were one. She could feel them being transported by that kiss, taken to that place she knew was the Light.

She gasped as suddenly she saw the snow-capped mountains of Colorado rise up like a vision, and then she was on the hard ground of the foothills, her mate on top of her, kissing her deep, kissing her hard, kissing her with everything he had.

"Ohmygod," she managed to whisper as she broke from his kiss long enough to take in the scent of the wild mountains she'd loved as a child, as a kitten, as a girl discovering who she was. A girl who was now a woman. A woman who'd just saved the world!

She arched her back as Everett dragged his tongue down along her bare neck, pushing his face between her breasts and breathing deep like he wanted to inhale her. She could smell his masculine scent strong in the crisp air, and she moaned as Everett coated her breasts with his saliva like he was marking her as his, his alone.

"I want to eat you up," he growled, raising his head and grinning at her. He raised an eyebrow and then shrugged. "In fact, I think I *will* eat you up!"

Tracy squealed as Everett opened his mouth and took her left nipple between his lips, sucking so hard she thought he actually might swallow her whole! His hands were beneath her, cupping her ass and squeezing with the strength of his tiger, fingers digging into her flesh as he sucked her boobs until both nipples were pert and sharp like arrowheads. A moment later he was kissing her round belly, tickling her belly-button with his tongue, coating her all over with his tiger's mark, claiming her in her beloved mountains, where she was most comfortable, where she was herself.

"This is all I want," he whispered against her glistening stomach, his breath hot like fire against her skin. "You. Every part of you, Tracy. Inside and outside."

Tracy felt her wetness flow out of her as he spoke, and then Everett was between her legs, his face pushing deep into her triangle, his lips kissing her lips, his tongue sliding past her opening and curling up against the front wall of her vagina.

"Oh, shit," she groaned, her eyes rolling up in her head as Everett dragged his stiff tongue along her inner walls, rolling it around like he wanted to taste every inch of her secret space. She was so wet it felt like a river flowing from her, and she groaned again as she heard her mate slurp and swallow like he was drinking from a mountain spring.

"You taste so good," he whispered, his voice thick with ecstasy. Her eyelids were fluttering as the ecstasy rolled through her body in waves, and it took a moment before she could focus enough to look at him. "Here. Taste yourself."

With a mischievous grin he rose up and smacked her lips, forcing her to taste her own juices. His heavy cock pressed down on her mound as he lay on top of her, and the sensation of his hardness on her clit made Tracy open her mouth wide.

"Salty," she muttered with a smile. "Is that really what I taste like?"

"You taste sweet like honey," he said with a grin. "What do I taste like?"

Tracy blinked, and then she gasped again as Everett kissed her gently and then leaned back, straddling her carefully before leaning back again until his cock stood straight out over her breasts like a log. She took a moment to just stare, feeling herself close to climax just from the sight of his thick shaft, its red tip shining with his clean oil, drops of his pre-cum falling on her naked nipples like dewdrops at dawn. Everett's face was twisted with need, and he groaned as he lowered his cockhead to her left nipple, coating the erect nub with his natural juice. He dragged his cock along the curve of her breasts, down through the valley between her rises, marking her other nipple before leaning back again.

"Oh, God, Everett," Tracy whimpered when she saw the arousal marking his handsome face. "Come here. Bring it here. Let me taste you."

She reached out and gripped his cock by the shaft, groaning when she saw that her fingers didn't even go all the way around, he was so damned thick. With her other hand she cupped his balls, marveling at how heavy they were, her mind clouding over as her pussy tightened like it was yearning to feel him empty himself into her.

"Bloody hell, that feels so good, Tracy," he growled, his eyes rolling up in his head as Tracy stroked him, massaging his balls gently as she lov-

ingly jerked his foreskin to and fro. She watched
how his lean, hard abs tensed up with her touch,
how those muscles on his massive chest tightened
and released as she brought him closer to climax.

Tracy smiled as she imagined Everett exploding all over her, coating her breasts with his thick
semen. The thought made her own wetness flow
so hard she could feel it pool on the ground beneath her ass. She smiled as she pulled his cock
closer to her mouth, kissing his red tip, rolling her
tongue all over his cockhead until Everett arched
his head back and roared like the tiger he was.

Above him the magical skies looked like they
were darkening, and Tracy smiled wider as she
felt her heat rise. Slowly she drew Everett into
her mouth, opening her throat as he pushed himself in, deep in, all the way in until his balls were
against her damned chin!

"Bloody hell," he muttered again, holding her
head in his big hands, fingers curling her hair and
pulling until she could feel her roots screaming
with the most wonderful pain. Everything had
been gentle and slow thus far, but as the skies
turned to a deep purple and the Light began to
fade to Darkness, she knew the animal in her
mate was coming out.

She was going to bring out the animal in him.

With all her might Tracy sucked, her eyes almost popping out of her head as Everett roared again and pushed down her throat so deep she thought she might choke! Then he was fucking her in the mouth, his thrusts going harder as she sucked and swallowed, her entire body shaking as Everett held her head in place and slid his mighty cock in and out until her chin was dripping with saliva and his pre-cum.

Above them dark clouds were forming, and Tracy could feel their arousal taking them to that place where animal lust reigned supreme. But it didn't feel ominous or threatening. She understood that balance didn't mean equilibrium. It meant they could take each other to the edges, to the extremes, to the boundaries!

They could make gentle love in the brightest part of the Light.

And they could fuck like beasts in the darkest depths of the Night.

Tracy screamed as the skies suddenly turned full black, and Everett roared as he pulled his cock out of her mouth and flipped her over like a ragdoll, his tremendous strength making her scream again.

He grabbed her from behind, raising her hips and smacking her upturned ass twice on each cheek, the slaps sounding like whipcracks, the sting of his hands on her flesh making her shriek. Again he spanked her bum, roaring like the animal he was as she howled and purred and moaned from the depths of the animal *she* was! In her mind's eye she could see the marks his fingers were leaving on her broad buttocks, and she smiled as she realized he was marking her again, this time from the animal in him, the Darkness in him. It felt as pure and natural as when they'd lovingly tasted each other in the Light, lovingly marked each other in her safe place in the mountains, her feminine wetness coating his face, his masculine juice painting her body like a canvas.

Everett spanked her three more times on each cheek, and then grabbed her ass with both hands when he was done. He stretched her buttcheeks wide, holding them spread open as Tracy gasped at the feeling of his hot breath against her open rear hole.

"Dark and beautiful," he whispered against her rear, kissing the inside curves of her buttocks. "So fucking beautiful."

Tracy felt herself come just from his words, just from how his breath felt against her crack, just from how beautifully filthy it all felt. She groaned as her orgasm slowly wound its way through her like a snake, her pussy dripping as Everett's tongue circled her rim until she knew she was shining with his wetness.

He licked her from behind as she came again, came from the inside, without him even touching her clit. Her climax was as mental as it was physical, and she understood how Dark and Light were finding their meeting place within her, within her body, within her soul, within her union with her mate.

Everett's tongue slid into her rear just as Tracy's climax hit its peak, and she almost cried with pleasure as he pushed his face so deep between her cheeks it was like he was trying to climb up inside her, enter her fully, consume her, possess her!

He pulled his face back after several long moments of the most divinely filthy licking, and then his fingers were inside her rear, two fingers, three, finally four!

"Oh, fuck, Everett!" she cried out, her mouth opening wide as he stretched her rear pucker, massaging that tight opening, spreading his fingers as he prepared her to take him. "Oh, please, Everett. *Please!*"

"Now you're learning some manners, Eliza," he

growled devilishly against her back, the fingers of his other hand spreading her slit from below, entering her quickly and expertly, driving back and forth almost immediately.

Tracy just gurgled as her vision blurred and her head spun. She was being fingered in both holes at once, and it was all she could do to not pass out from the dark ecstasy that was making her blood throb in her veins like she was close to exploding. She came again as he fucked her with his fingers, and then just as she thought she couldn't handle any more, with four fingers still deep in her anus, Everett held her slit open, let out a low, beastly grunt, and pushed his cock up into her pussy from behind, all the way deep, all the damned way.

"Bloody hell," Tracy gurgled, her throat closing up as she felt the full girth of her mate spread her so wide, his length driving up into her with such force she thought he'd split her down the middle. "Oh, bloody hell."

17

Bloody hell, Everett thought as he felt the skies darken behind him, felt the animal need in him come alive as Tracy sucked him to the point where he thought he'd explode. He'd lost himself in her after that, completely lost himself to her. She was bringing out parts of him he didn't know existed, parts of his need that he understood came from the animal, from the darkest part of the animal.

"Dark and beautiful," he'd heard himself whisper after spanking her big beautiful bum and spreading her shuddering asscheeks so wide he thought he might rip her apart. The sight of her rear pucker was almost too much for him, its clean circle shining with dark light that he was certain was magic, pure fucking magic.

She'd tasted divine, both from outside and inside. She'd smelled clean and warm, like a woman in need, like an animal in heat. And finally when he'd pushed his cock into her magnificent cunt, she'd tightened around his girth like she'd been made for him, just for him, all his, always his.

"You're mine, Tracy," he growled as he pumped into her, watching his long, glistening cock emerge from between her thighs before he rammed back into her again. "My bobcat. My woman. My mate."

"All yours, Everett," she gurgled from beneath him, her voice lilting from the way he was pounding her body with his powerful hips. Her ass was spread wide before him, his fingers firmly pushed inside her rear like he was holding her in place. He could feel her sex dripping down his cock, coating his balls, flowing down his goddamn thighs. When he glanced down he could see their combined juices gleaming on the invisible ground like black diamonds, and he roared as he felt his tiger's frenzy in the background, sensed Tracy's bobcat mewling as its human was taken.

Taken by the tiger.

And then suddenly Everett came, his balls seizing up as he pushed his cock so far inside her that his hips were jammed between her spread buttocks. He knew that Tracy had been climaxing for a while, but he felt her pussy clench around him as he blasted the first of his load into her warm depths, her body tightening as another orgasm slammed into her like a freight train.

Everett shouted as he poured his load into her, his cock feeling like a fireman's hose gone wild, his balls serving up so much semen he thought he'd fill up his woman until she overflowed! One look down and Everett shouted again when he saw that hell, she *was* overflowing, her pussy oozing his thick semen even as she milked more out of him!

He felt Tracy reach beneath herself and clutch his balls, massaging them with her soft palms, coaxing more and more out of him. He wasn't sure if he was dreaming, but it felt like he could come forever. Perhaps he *would* come forever! An endless orgasm!

He looked down at his quivering mate, taking

in her strong hourglass shape spread before him in the darkness of their magical bed amongst the stars. Then he pulled out of her, spanked her buttocks once more, and without hesitation slid his still-spurting cock deep into her asshole!

"Oh, *shit!*" she howled, turning her head halfway, her eyes going wide with the shock of his entry. Then her shoulders hunched up, her hair hung down, and she just braced herself as Everett started pumping, somehow sustaining that orgasm, his balls swinging like heavy bags against her underside as he unloaded into her rear canal until she was once again overflowing!

They fucked like animals for what seemed like hours, months, perhaps years, and finally Everett pulled out of her, watching in amazement as his cock spurted one last load all over her smooth lower back before he collapsed on top of her.

They lay in silence, Everett covering his mate like a blanket, his cock pressed between them, still heavy like a log. At first there was no sound except for their heavy breathing.

But then he heard it.

Their hearts.

Their hearts, beating as one, in perfect rhythm, with perfect synchronicity, a rhythm in tune with the thrum of the universe.

"I love you, Tracy," Everett whispered into her hair even as he felt the skies lighten like a new day was dawning.

"I love you too," she said, her voice trembling before she returned to that peaceful silence of their heartbeats. Then a moment later she grunted, like she'd just realized she was leaking all over! "Damn right, you love me! I'm overflowing with your seed, you beast," she said. She tried to turn her head, but Everett was too exhausted to move off her.

Finally Everett looked down between them, glancing at her ass and grunting. "Yes, you are overflowing. I might have to wait a few minutes before going again." He grunted again as she giggled. "And you took an awfully long time to say you love me back, by the way. Very romantic. I shoulda known better than to pick an American as a mate."

"First of all," Tracy said, wriggling beneath him and finally managing to turn, "you didn't *pick* me as a mate. And second of all, *shoulda* is not a word in the English language."

"I shoulda filled your mouth too," Everett muttered, raising an eyebrow. Then he shrugged. "You know, maybe I will!"

"Ohmygod, you will *not*!" Tracy squealed as

Everett straddled her and grasped his cock with both hands, jerking himself back up to full hardness. "Get that thing away from my face, you . . . you *animal*!"

And as she said it her bobcat burst forth in an explosion of energy, and Tracy roared like the mountain lion she was, her sleek animal breaking away from Everett and racing away in playful glee!

"Oh no, you don't!" roared Everett, calling his Tiger, which came forth with delight, its massive body bursting through the man, its muscular haunches flexing as it pushed off and gave chase, ready to chase its mate across the universe, the universe which was now their playground!

18

It's a magical playground, Tracy thought as she felt her bobcat run like the wind, its energy overflowing, its joy boundless from the frenzied coupling of its human with its mate. She'd been so overwhelmed with the joy of her cat that at first she hadn't noticed that the scenery had changed, that the darkness had given way to dawn, that she was now running on soft ground, along the

banks of a raging river, the smell of wet mud filling her senses, the sound of the rapids like nature's music!

She raced around a set of rocks, following the
river downhill, feeling her tiger hot on her heels,
sensing the big beast's joy and playfulness. She
knew Everett's tiger could catch her anytime he
wanted. It could run her down in a flash, over-
power her in an instant, do with her what it wanted. But all it wanted to do right now was play,
she understood. The sexual energy had smoothly
transformed into the simple energy of animals at
play, and she howled in delight as Everett swatted
her with a mighty paw, sending her bobcat rolling
head over heels but in a perfectly controlled way!

The two cats played like they didn't have a care
in the world, barreling their way through bush-
es that sprung up out of nowhere, climbing up
low-rising trees and leaping off branches onto
the soft grass. Soon Tracy realized they were
creating their surroundings as they played, and
when she saw her beautiful mountains in the
distance even as Everett chased her through the
yellow-gold elephant grass of his beloved Savannah, she understood that they were creating this
reality together.

Finally they tumbled over each other at the edge of a clearing, the two cats panting in excitement as they lay on their bellies, nuzzling against one another, licking each other's snouts, both of them with big, dopey grins as a love pure and simple flowed through them like that distant river.

"We really *can* travel through Light and Dark together!" Tracy said, her voice bubbling with excitement. "And it's all beautiful, isn't it? It's all perfect!"

"It *is* perfect," said Everett, his tiger's eyes beaming as he surveyed the surroundings and then settled his gaze on her. "A perfect ending."

"A perfect ending," Tracy repeated, her voice coming out as a murmur. She blinked as a flickering image of her sister came to her mind. But she knew Lacy was happy. Lacy was back in the world of flesh and blood, joined forever with her mate Darius. Hell, she was probably giving birth to their kittens right now!

The thought of kittens sparked something in Tracy, and before she could blink again she realized she'd Changed back to the woman. She looked down at herself, and when she looked back up, she saw that Everett had Changed back too, once he'd seen her Change.

"What?" he said. "Did I say something? I didn't mean this is the end. It's just as accurate to say that it's the beginning! The beginning of our forever!"

"No, it's not that," Tracy muttered, drawing her knees up to her body and hugging herself. It took some effort to actually hug herself, and Tracy frowned again as she wondered if she'd somehow gotten fatter even though she didn't remember eating anything in the afterlife. "Um, do my boobs look bigger to you?" she said as she stared down at herself.

"Is that a trick question?" said Everett with a grin.

"No, I'm serious, you oaf!" said Tracy straightening up and gasping when she felt how heavy her boobs were. Heavy and full. "Here, feel them! They're heavy, Everett!"

"If this is a trick, then I'm falling for it," growled Everett, leaning close and grasping her breasts, one in each hand. Slowly he squeezed, groaning softly as his cock stood straight up. He played with her nipples a bit, pinching harder and harder until he was roughly plucking and pulling at her stiff nubs.

And then it happened. Her nipples tightened, and she squirted a shot of white milk directly up into Everett's face!

"Ow!" Everett roared, turning his face away and then looking at her in shock. He licked his lips, and then broke into a surprised smile. "I mean, wow!"

"It can't be," Tracy muttered, shaking her head as she looked down at her boobs and realized they were heavy with milk! Breast milk! Mommy's milk! "Ohmygod, Everett! Look!"

They both looked down past her oozing breasts, and Tracy gasped when she saw how distended her belly had gotten! She'd always had a gut, but this was different. This was . . . she was . . .

"Pregnant?" she whispered as that vision of her seven unborn kittens came back to her like they were mewling out loud! She'd had that vision earlier, but although it had seemed real, she'd decided that it had to be imagination. After all, they were both dead, weren't they? They hadn't had intercourse before they died. Could she actually have gotten pregnant in the afterlife? Could she give birth here?

Both joy and panic whipped through her at

once as Everett pulled her close and held her. She knew he was experiencing the same confusion, the same happiness, the same feeling of WTF?!

"Yes," Everett finally said, his eyes shining as he cupped her face in his big hands and gave a her warm, wet kiss. "Why not! We're both body and spirit out here, aren't we? We can travel between Darkness and Light. We're bonded mates. Why *can't* we have babies in this place? Your sister was pregnant while she was here with us, wasn't she?"

"Yeah, but Lacy had gotten knocked up *before* she and Darius killed themselves to come find us," Tracy said, frowning as she tried to put her finger on what seemed wrong about this whole situation.

Nothing is wrong, whispered her bobcat from inside her, its voice coming out like a snarl. *You're about to give birth to our kittens. Now lean back, spread your legs, and push. Push, dammit! PUSH!*

19

PUSH!

Everett was startled to hear his tiger growl out the word. Then he realized his tiger was trying to talk directly to Tracy even though Everett was in human form! The animal was yearning to see its kittens pop out of Tracy, and Everett had to grit his teeth to force his tiger to the background again!

You can't stop it, his tiger growled. *It's too late.*

Our kittens are coming, and we will raise them here, in this realm where the tiger rules supreme.

"What the hell are you talking about?" whispered Everett to his animal as he watched Tracy lean back and scream like she was going into labor. "Tracy! Hold on! I'm here, baby! I'm here!"

We're all here, whispered his tiger. *And we'll always be here. Once our kittens are born, there'll be no going back. They will be of this world, this greater world, born with the ability to travel between Light and Darkness, the ability to treat the cosmos as their playground. They will be gods. Cat gods.*

Everett's mind raced as he cradled his screaming mate against his chest and tried to figure out what was happening. He understood that time worked differently in this place, that even though it seemed like only a few days had passed, it could have been years in Earth time! After all, Tracy's sister had to return to the world in time to give birth, nine months passing in just a few hours! So yes, time meant nothing out here!

He listened to his tiger go on and on about the tiger's destiny, the tiger's powers, and as Everett thought back to the volumes of mythology he'd read as a graduate student, something stuck out to him:

"In Asian mythology the Tiger is the only beast that can rival the Dragon," he muttered aloud, petting Tracy's hair, dabbing the sweat off her forehead as she began to hyperventilate. "The only beast that can*kill* a dragon!"

The moment he voiced the thought, a bloodcurdling screech filled the air, and suddenly Everett realized that the sky was gone, the sun was gone, the light was gone! Was he back in the Darkness? So what if he was? The Darkness was no threat now that they were bonded!

But then the screech came again, and when Everett managed to get his tiger under enough control to use its night-vision, he roared out loud when he saw the glistening walls of Sinesta's dragon-belly pulsating around them!

"We're still inside the dragon!" he shouted, shaking Tracy back to her senses. But she was still hyperventilating, her legs spread wide as if she was about to give birth! "Of course we're still inside the dragon's belly," Everett growled, shaking his head, furious at himself. "If we'd really been coughed out, we'd have found ourselves back in the world of flesh and blood, not prancing about the universe like carefree kittens! Everything we experienced was real, but also an illusion. We thought we could live here in this greater reality, and in our ecstasy we forgot that the Shifter's place is on Earth, that it can only find everlasting balance in the world of flesh and blood." Again he looked down at his mate, cradling her face and leaning close. "You can't give birth here, Tracy. If you do, our kittens will be born having never experienced life in flesh and blood! They won't be true Shifters! Ignore whatever your animal is saying, Tracy! It's blind to the greater purpose of the Shifter spirit. It senses that its kittens are close, and that's all it cares about. It doesn't understand what it means in the long run. We have to go back to the world, Tracy. We have to go back to the physical. For us. For our children. And perhaps for the world itself. We have to go back!"

20

"**Y**ou have to come back!" came Lacy's voice through Tracy's pain, through the mewling of her bobcat, which was trying desperately to push its kittens out into this no-man's land. "We've been trying to find you for years, Tracy! We thought we'd lost you forever! You need to come back! We're losing the battle here! We need you and the tiger to complete Magda's circle of power, to give her magic the energy she needs to stop Sinesta!"

"*Stop* Sinesta?" said Tracy, feeling the sweat roll down her cheeks as Everett stroked her hair. "But . . . but we *saved* Sinesta! We put her back together! Reunited the splintered parts of her soul with her dragon!*Murad* was the threat! A threat we should have neutralized once the she-Dragon's balance was restored!"

"Except the she-Dragon's balance *wasn't* restored!" snapped Lacy, and now Tracy could see her sister's face clearly in her vision, a vision tinged with dark red like it was bleeding!

Lacy looked like she'd aged, but not in a natural way. She had lines on her face that shouldn't be there. Her eyes were bloodshot and weary. In the background Tracy could see Lacy's kittens, and she gasped when she saw that the kids were walking upright already.

"Ohmygod, how many years has it been?!" Tracy shrieked.

"Five years, you moron!" said Lacy, finally smiling, her eyes tearing up. "Five years we've been trying to stop Sinesta, but her rage is only growing."

"I . . . I still don't get it," Tracy stammered.

"When the dragon swallowed us it said it was seeking balance, that it was all Darkness and so it was yearning to devour Light! It said reuniting it with its human would bring it balance! We went to the Light and found Sinesta's human soul, Lacy! We dragged it back to its dragon! Reunited the dark dragon with the Light of its human!"

"Except Sinesta's human soul had lost its Light," came Magda's voice, and Tracy blinked as the dark witch's face came through clear. "And that was the dragon's last hope at finding balance. When it emerged into the world, its fury was unbridled. Its need to devour Light was like an unquenchable thirst. It was full of hate, madness, the need for revenge. It killed Murad over the Mediterranean Sea, blasting him out of the skies with fire so hot the sea itself started to boil! And then it went on a rampage, devouring humans in its savage quest to consume Light! Human souls must have looked like specks of Light to the mad dragon."

"Five years?!" Tracy gasped. "But wouldn't it have destroyed the world by now? Eaten every human on Earth?"

"It would have, but a year ago it calmed down suddenly," said Magda, squinting as if she could see Tracy. "Wait, are you . . . is that . . . oh, God, Tracy! That's it! That's why Sinesta has calmed down! It feels you giving birth inside its belly!"

"What?" Tracy muttered, blinking as she looked down at herself and then at her surroundings. It was only then that she realized they were back inside Sinesta's belly! What the hell?! "Why?"

"I don't know why," said Magda, her eyes darting left and right in despair. "I can't see into Sinesta's soul. I don't know what's driving her."

"I do," Tracy whispered, a sudden clarity coming to her out of nowhere. "I've looked into Sinesta's eyes, Magda. I'm the *only* one who's looked into Sinesta's eyes. I've seen why her human soul lost its Light. I understand why the feeling of giving birth would bring the Light back. She's a mother, Magda. A mother who turned on her child and never forgave herself for it. She thought she could let go of it on that slice of heaven, that she could dance away from all the worries of the flesh. But she couldn't. Heaven isn't an escape route. You don't get to run away from yourself, from your conscience, from your soul."

"Nobody's running away," came Everett's voice. But the voice was deep, throaty, and when Tracy turned to her mate, she saw he'd Changed to his Tiger! "This ends now. It ends in blood."

"What are you doing?!" Tracy screamed as Everett went up on his hind legs, his massive claws shining in the eerie darkness, his jaws opening wide as he faced the living walls of Sinesta's belly!

"The Tiger is the only beast that can kill a dragon," Everett roared, his eyes blazing with his beast's power. "There's no hope for Sinesta to regain balance in the world of flesh and blood. And I'm sure as hell not letting you give birth to our kittens in her goddamn belly! Her mate killed her in the flesh. When she returned to the flesh, she killed her mate in return! These two overgrown lizards deserve each other, Tracy. Let them roam the universe together for eternity! Let them join our own parents, all of whom made choices that defined their future."

"And our choices will define *our* future!" Tracy screamed, feeling her bobcat again try to push out its kittens. "We have to choose life, not death! This is all a test, Everett!" She turned to that vision of Magda. "What happens if I give birth here, Magda? Will my kittens die? Will they be consumed by the dragon in its quest for Light?

And if Everett and I return to the world, will our
kittens come with us, or will they be left behind?"

Magda's eyes were wide, and she just shook her
head. "I . . . I don't know, Tracy. Oh, God, I just
don't know!"

Tracy once again felt the pressure of her impending delivery, and she groaned as she thought
her head might explode. Suddenly she realized
it was all on her. Everything depending on her
choice. She'd always been the younger sister, pro-
tected and coddled. Now she was about to be a
mother, about to make a choice that might save
the world but sacrifice her kittens!

She looked up at her mate, a Tiger blazing orange and black, claws of deadly gold, teeth of
gleaming ivory. It looked frozen in time—in
fact everything looked frozen, like the spin of the
universe itself was waiting for Tracy to decide
what to do next!

Tracy cocked her head and frowned as she
looked at the Tiger. Didn't it want to see its kittens born, just like her bobcat was yearning for
her to push them out of her womb? Did its blood-
lust overrule the need to see its own offspring
come into being?

No, she realized with a slow smile. It's Everett the man controlling his animal, redirecting its energy towards violence, giving me time to make my decision! The Tiger wants to see its kittens born, but Everett believes that I shouldn't give birth in this place. I want to do what my mate wants, what my man wants. But I also believe that our animals have a right to want what *they* want! That was the whole point of everything we've gone through, wasn't it? The whole point of everything we've *all* gone through!

Tracy felt a lazy smile break on her face, and as the tears rolled down her cheeks, she saw everything laid out before her, all the couples that had come together, fated mates fighting to find balance within themselves, within each other, then as a crew, finally turning their attention outward in an effort to bring balance to the world itself. Everything had built up to this moment, and Tracy nodded as the answer came to her.

She had to find a way to balance everything. The needs of their animals, the needs of their humans, the joy of the Light, the pull of the Darkness.

"Sinesta is not some ghoul or demon that wants

to devour our newborns," Tracy said, thinking aloud as the Tiger moved in a slow motion attack. "She just needs to regain that feeling of childbirth, something that was made dark and violent for her because she was killed while giving birth. She just needs to feel it, and the Light will return to her. She'll understand that a mother's fate is to love her child, good or bad, monster or saint, human or beast. So I'll share that feeling with her. Mother to mother. Remind her what it feels like to be a mother. How the love of a parent for a child is what humans and animals have in common, will always have in common."

She nodded as she made her choice, relaxing her body and gasping as she felt her kittens slide out of her with ease as natural as riverflow, as beautiful as birdsong, as perfect as any picture of paradise. She saw Everett roar in the background, his claws about to rip into Sinesta's body from the inside.

Then she felt Sinesta . . . really *felt* her.

And she knew she'd made the right choice.

Tracy wept as she felt Sinesta getting put back together by what was playing out in slow motion in the theater of her belly, in her own womb, with Everett's tiger playing the role of the monster in

Sinesta's belly while Tracy shared the beauty of childbirth with Sinesta's ravaged soul.

She wept as she heard Sinesta's dragon wail in horror as Everett's claws pierced its flesh.

She wept as she felt Sinesta's human cry out in joy as Tracy pushed out the last of her seven kittens.

And then she wept when everything froze again, the Tiger turning away from its attack to gaze upon its newborns, Everett the man unable to stop himself from basking in the beauty of fresh fatherhood.

"What have you done?" he screamed, Changing back to the man and dropping to his knees, gathering his mate and their seven kittens in his big hands. "Tracy, if they're born here, they won't be able to go back to the world with us!"

"They aren't born yet," Tracy said, smiling as she looked down at the glistening cord that still connected her babies to her body, an umbilical cord that was glowing with energy of both Light and Dark, branching out in seven directions all at once. "They're gonna go where we go. Now hold on. We're about to get—"

But her words were lost as a rush of sea air blasted them, and with a scream Tracy felt them being pulled up along the dragon's gullet like they were on a slip-n-slide!

"Wheee!" she screamed, watching her kittens get pulled along with her, her mate desperately trying to hold them even though Tracy knew they would be safe, that the cord wasn't breaking. "Look! No hands!"

21

Everett pushed himself up with his hands, coughing out a mouthful of sand as he took gulping breaths and squinted in the sunlight of the Moroccan coast. He was naked and wet, and he felt the need to roar out loud, like he'd just been born himself!

Desperately he looked around for his mate and kittens, almost collapsing in relief when he saw them alive and safe on the beach just a few feet away. All seven kittens were clinging to Mommy like little monkeys, fighting for access to her big red nipples, which were oozing with fresh milk.

"About time Daddy woke up," said Tracy with a smile.

"What?" said Everett, grinning as he clambered over to his family, kicking away a big rock, tossing a fat crab out of his path. "How long was I out?"

"Five years," said Tracy without missing a beat. "Talk about being a deadbeat dad. I know I should-nta married a head-in-the-clouds intellectual. But that Tiger's butt is mighty hard to turn down."

Everett swallowed hard before bursting into laughter. "*Shouldnta*? That's a travesty even for an uneducated American mountain-girl." He kissed her on the forehead before bending down and kissing each one of his new babies, four girls and a triple-set of boys. One of them tried to bite his nose, perhaps thinking it was a nipple, and Everett growled playfully at his son before kissing his mate again. "Wait, did you say married? Did you make me sign something while I was passed out?"

Tracy laughed and shook her head, and Everett was about to kiss her again when the sound of wings and the scent of Shifter blood made him jump to his feet, ready to Change into his Tiger in case he needed to protect his family.

He stared up into the skies, tensing up as the massive outline of a flying dragon popped into view.

"Sinesta," he growled. "You should've let me finish her off when I had the chance. Now get back behind those rocks. Protect our children. Don't come out until it's over." He turned to her fiercely. "Until it's over, you hear? No matter which one of us is left standing."

"My, aren't we feeling heroic! What are you, some mythical beast in a Greek epic? This is a romance story, not a tragedy!" Tracy rolled her eyes as she sniffed the air and shook her head. "You're losing your sense of smell in your old age, honey. That's not Sinesta." She sniffed the air again as the dragon grew close enough for them to make out some shadowy figures on the dragon's massive back. "That's our happy ending, Everett. What does it smell like?"

"Smells like a bunch of mangy furballs riding an overgrown lizard," growled Everett, his heart leaping as he watched Adam Drake's green-and-gold dragon swoop in for a landing. On his back was a cluster of Shifters, all of them in animal form, all of them grinning wide as they leapt off Adam's back and raced over to Everett and Tracy.

"Careful who you call mangy," said Darius the lion, sniffing Everett and pretending to turn up his nose. "You smell like seawater that just got puked up by a dragon."

Everyone laughed, and then the crew of Shifters gathered around Tracy and her kittens, each one welcoming the newest members of their extended family: Ash and Bart the sibling Bears; Bismeeta the Leopard; Caleb the Wolf; Magda the Fox; Darius the Lion; and of course, Lacy the bobcat.

"Speaking of dragons," Everett said after the cooing and purring and cuddling had died down enough for him to get a word in. He turned to the open sea and scanned the horizon. "Where's Sinesta?" He looked around and frowned. "And where the hell did Adam go?"

"He needs a moment," said Ash, Adam's Bear-Shifter mate. "A family moment."

Suddenly the skies went dark, and Everett craned his neck upwards, once again standing over his mate and kittens in a protective stance. "Holy mother of God," he muttered, staring along with the rest of the Shifters as they watched Adam's green-and-gold dragon glide through the skies.

Behind Adam flew two young dragons, one green and one gold, both of them flying strong and hard, in perfect formation behind their father . . . flying directly towards their grandmother!

"Sinesta!" Tracy whispered, clutching her heart as she felt the love in the air, the love of a mother reuniting with her son, seeing her own grandchildren for the first time. "Oh God, Everett! Isn't it beautiful?"

Everett felt a lump in his throat as he sank down into the sand, pulling his mate and children so close he could hear all their hearts beating together. He lay his head back, letting the beauty of the moment sink in as he watched Sinesta fly alongside her son, shoot friendly little fireballs at her grandchildren until they screeched in pleasure. The dragons dipped and dived together, rose up to where they looked like specks, descended back down with screaming speed, pulling up just before hitting the ocean, the force of their afterburn sending waves crashing into the shore, splashing all of the laughing Shifters with warm surf!

"Bloody overgrown lizards," Everett muttered, but although he tried to sound aloof, he couldn't hold back the true emotion in his voice, and Tracy just looked up at him and cuddled closer to her mate. They lay together and watched the show of dragon-love unfolding in the skies above, but then Everett frowned as he saw Sinesta's wings flicker with light.

"What's happening?" said Tracy, frowning and then turning toward Magda. Immediately Tracy went quiet, her body relaxing with a strange sigh.

Everett felt the hush ripple through all the Shifters, and then he heard Magda's voice. It was a low whisper. Words he couldn't understand.

Then he understood.

The circle was complete. Each Shifter with its true mate. Each Shifter with a complete bond, their animals in perfect balance, happy with having found their fated mates and producing their offspring. Magda's magic now had the power she needed, and she was sending Sinesta back to where she belonged.

Back to her true mate.

"Sinesta's dragon was never part of this world," Magda said in a low voice when the spell was complete and Sinesta faded into the distance like a song approaching the end. "Its fury at its mate has been satisfied, and now it is free to live in eternity with its true match."

"Brutal," said Everett grimly, folding his hands as he watched Adam's dragon screech out a good-bye high above them.

"Why, thank you, brother," said Bart the Bear, breaking the sadness with a quip that made them all laugh.

Of course, they laughed because they all knew there was truth in what Bart had just said. A Shifter's nature *was* brutal. But so was the universe's nature, wasn't it? The universe's energy was an energy of eternal destruction, wasn't it? Death of the old. Birth of the new.

Tracy nodded as she looked up into the stars, glancing back down at her Shifter friends and family and then back up at the heavens. They'd all lost parents to what lay out there. But they had all been blessed with new life. New life that was connected to the old.

A cosmic circle that would keep on spinning.

Spinning forever.

Always and forever.

∞

The End.

EPILOGUE

"**T**his isn't the end of it, you goddamn lizard!" roared Bart the Bear, struggling wildly against the magic-infused chains that were holding his massive body pinned down in his chair. "I just wanted to go to the bathroom!"

Adam snorted, standing up from the long dinner table in the Great Hall of his lair in the Caspian Sea. All the Shifters giggled as Tracy and Everett stared in wonder. Adam nodded at Magda, as if thanking her for trapping Bart the Bear. Then he turned to Everett and Tracy, letting out a slow sigh and reaching beneath the table.

"Bathroom, my ass," Adam grunted, smiling at Bart as he placed a small box on the wooden tabletop, flipping it open to reveal a massive diamond ring. "I know what you were going for, and I refuse to replace my vault doors again."

"You stingy bastard!" Bart growled, his eyes twinkling with mischief. "Can't escape those dragon's hoarding instincts, can you? That rock's the size of a peanut! Let me go down there and select one for our newest couple!"

Tracy stared at the massive jewel, blinking in astonishment when she realized that it was a gift from Adam to Everett . . . a gift from an Alpha to the newest member of his crew, his family!

"Um, that's plenty big," Tracy squealed, her voice coming out like a squeak. And it *was* big. Closer to a grapefruit than a peanut! She glanced over at Everett, wondering if he was going to make a wisecrack about her grammar. But she could see he was touched by Adam's gesture. He'd never had a brother. Never run with a pack or had a tribe. This was new to him. New, and deeply meaningful.

"You know," said Ash sweetly, touching Adam's hand and gesturing towards her chained-up brother Bart. "Bart's selected every other ring for the women in our crew. It almost seems like tradition now. Let him do it, hon. Come on."

Adam closed his eyes and exhaled, and Tracy gasped when she saw wisps of smoke come out of his nostrils. Shit, that whole hoarding-instinct thing was real, wasn't it?!

"All right," Adam said through gritted teeth. He nodded to Magda, who waved her hand and released Bart from the chains. "But let me open the vault for you this time. Just wait until I— Bart! *Bart!* My vaults! My *vaults!*"

But the bear barreled its way down the stairs so fast it seemed astounding for a creature that large, and Tracy had to control her laughter when she saw Adam turn purple with rage, sparks bursting from his nose, mouth, and even his ears. He roared in anger as they all heard a tremendous crash in the bowels of the castle.

"My vaults," Adam whispered in resignation, shaking his head as the bear came bounding back up, a diamond the size of a cantaloupe in his paw.

"All right, Tiger-boy," Bart grunted, tossing the ring to Everett and winking at Adam. "Do your thing while I calm Dragon-butt down."

Bart went over to his smoke-emitting Alpha, pulling him into a bear-hug that would have crushed any normal man—and even any normal Shifter. Finally Adam cooled down and just smiled, and then everyone went silent as Everett stood from the table, turned Tracy's chair around, went down on one knee, and asked the question that every other man in the room had done.

"Always and forever," Tracy said, just like every other woman in the room had once said to her mate. "Always and forever."

And everyone clapped as the universe took a snapshot of the moment, filing it away in Eternity's wedding album, sighing as it remembered that this was what it was all about.

All the drama.

All the madness.

Life and death.

Darkness and Light.

Love.

Just love.

Always.

And forever.

∞

FROM THE AUTHOR

This series took a lot out of me, and I hope you enjoyed it. Do let me know!

So sad to see these characters ride off into the sunset, but I can feel some more Shifters in our future! For now though, I'm going back to the real world (well, the Annabelle Winters version of the real world . . .).

I've got a super-hot contemporary series coming out: CURVY FOR HIM! Take a look!

Love,
Anna.

PS: And always, do consider my long, insanely hot series of full-length romances: CURVES FOR SHEIKHS.

Made in the USA
Las Vegas, NV
11 August 2023

75931551R00132